Lorelei the
Berserker

I0532826

BY BLUDGEON

This book is dedicated to the
friends whose encouragement,
enthusiasm, and help made
it possible. My gratitude
is eternal. Thank you.

Cover art by James Coats
Instagram @jacoats

Lorelei the Berserker is copyright ©2024,
Bludgeon. All rights reserved. No part of
this book may be reproduced without the
consent of the author.

ISBN: 978-1-7337639-4-3

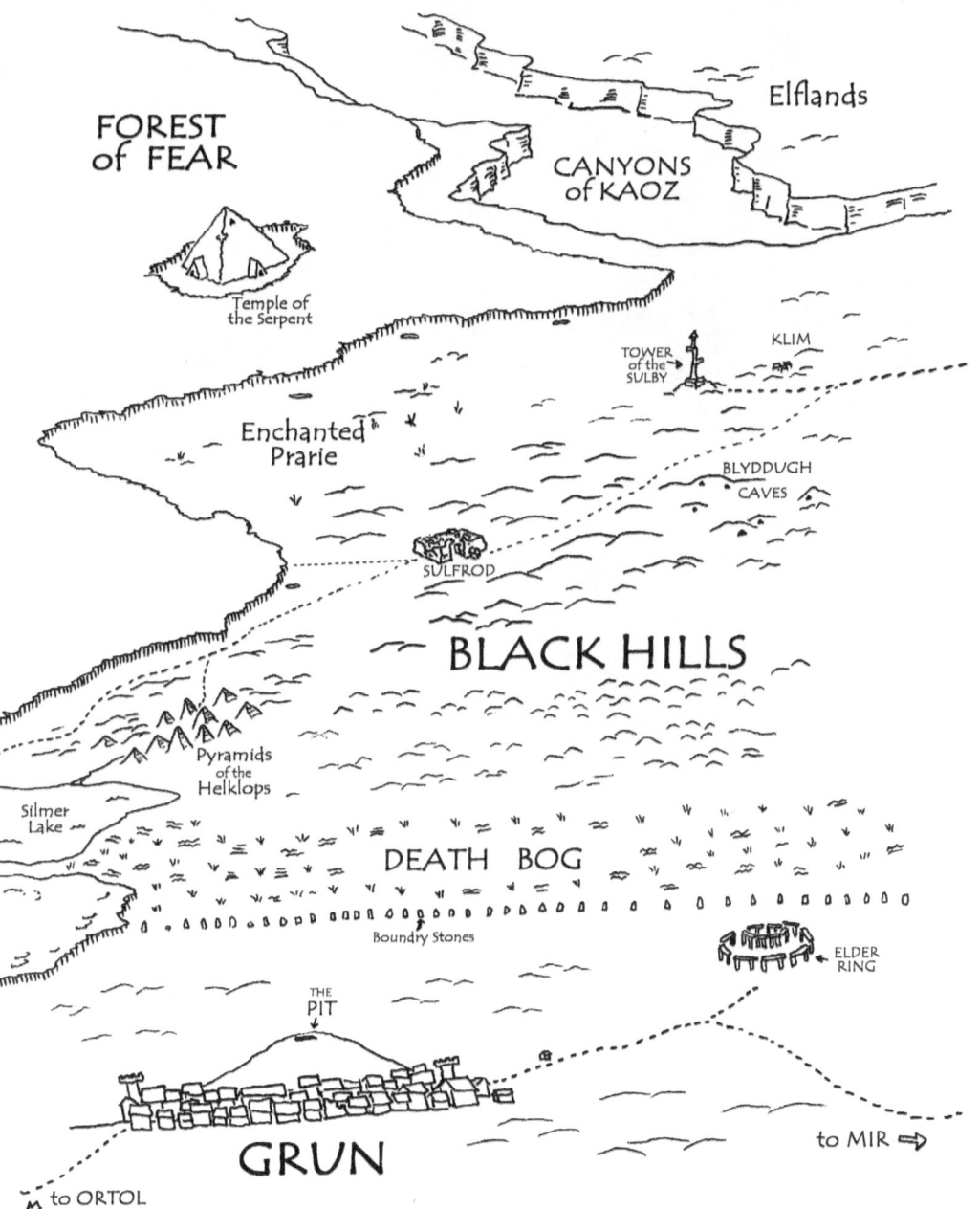

1. The Pit

There were no large city-centers in the vast untamed lands west of the treacherous triple rivers, colloquially known as the Demon's Tongue. But, in the north of one great valley full of heather-covered hills and scattered trees, miles from the nearest respectable town, was a notable village called Grun. Every week Grun would swell in size as people flocked to it from far and wide to partake in the excesses it provided, like flies swarming a rotten corpse. They came in caravans, wagons, and by horse and foot, frothing at the mouth, eager for some sort of release from their mundane lives. There were some who came, not for distraction, but commerce; seeking money-making opportunities and the information that flooded in with the wayfarers. Grun sat at an important crossroad and was frequented by many merchants, deal-makers, spies, thieves, and plotters of all sorts. The village itself was a mass of slightly crooked brick and timber buildings that encircled the base of a wide yet short hill with a very gentle rise and a broad flat top. A mix of great tents with flowing banners and small shacks with crude wooden signs covered the sides and top of the hill in an odd jumble that mirrored the intermingling menagerie of revelers hosted by the village each week. The openness of the fields around Grun allowed for a steady wind to blow across it and remove the lurid, suggestive, and disgusting smells that constantly accumulated on the hill. Re-enacted every six days, Grun played host to a two-day festival of hedonism and debauchery unmatched in all the western kingdoms. This notoriety brought many travelers, and much wealth, into Grun, and tonight's festivities were no different.

As the sun set, the sounds of music grew louder, the laughter increased, and as the air filled with excitement, a cloaked person with hood drawn up, passed through the cobblestone streets of Grun and began to climb the hill.

They had arrived two days prior but had preferred to camp in a field south of the village rather than mingle at an Inn with other travelers. This person was a woman, though it was impossible to tell as her dark cloak covered her whole body, while her face receded into the darkness that her hood provided. Her name was Lorelei. She walked with purpose among the tents and masses of uncouth revelers and was careful to avoid the strange puddles and little streams left by the crowds during their exuberant and volatile merrymaking. She kept her eyes forward and gave no heed to the spectacles she passed or the moans that lifted above the cheers and applause. At a glance, she seemed nothing more than a shadow moving amongst the mirth and writhing flesh. She was headed towards the very center of this debauched festival where, at the top of the hill, in the center of the great tents and shacks, stood an ancient stone-lined pit, where terrible games of violence were played out amidst a backdrop of cheers and laughter. Known far and wide, only the fiercest and most foolish fighters dared the brutality of the Pit of Grun, and that was exactly why Lorelei had come to this wasteland of a realm.

As she neared the top of the hill, the tents faded to leave only a swarming mass of humanity that laughed, cursed, and drank amidst its reek and vomit. The area was illuminated by dozens of large torches on poles and wide braziers on the ground, making sure no hedonistic acts went unseen. It was wild exuberance, drunkenness, and carnal desire; the likes of which Lorelei had never witnessed. Above the bouncing jubilant heads of the crowd, she could see two well-worn stone totems a good thirty feet apart. She assumed that these eldritch figures marked the entrances to the Pit. With a smirk, she pushed her way through the drunken revelers until she could see that a large table sat against the nearest totem. A robed man with a graying beard and a broad blue hat adorned with a peacock's feather held a book and scribbled furiously as he yelled and absently chatted with various people around him. This must be the Pit Master, thought Lorelei, and in a town built upon communal inhibition and famous for violence, he was the de facto Mayor and voice of authority.

She approached the Pit Master as he hurriedly wrote marks in his large book. He glanced at her quickly and before he could turn away, he was caught by her piercing green eyes and her cloaked form. She was clearly not part of the raucous crowd, but someone here to conduct business of some sort. The Pit Master closed his book and faced her. He could just make out her sharp clean chin and small nose under her large and luminous eyes.

"I am the Pit Master of Grun," he said with a small bow. "How might I assist you, my Lady?"

"I am here to fight in the Pit," said Lorelei. "You are expecting me."

"Uhm," stammered the Pit Master, momentarily at a loss for words.

"I am Lorelei from the Blue Isle," she said. "I sent a boy in advance to deliver my marker."

"Ah, yes," recovered the Pit Master. "He delivered it. Have you fought in pits before?"

"None such as this," purred Lorelei with a relaxed and almost detached tone.

"I see," he said tipping his head. "We have never had a fighter from the Blue Isle before."

"I expect not," said Lorelei. "It is small, covered with nothing but farmsteads and goat herds— an inconsequential place. Hardy folk they are, but not warlike, and they would blanch and die if they were to see the frivolities of Grun."

The Pit Master looked about, and the nearest merchants were studying the cloaked newcomer dubiously, shaking their heads. Like this throng of experienced gamblers, the Pit Master knew that women rarely entered the Pit, and when they did it made for poor and pitiful fights. In his many years as Master, only one woman had ever made a good showing in this crucible of murder and violence, and he was loth to allow another into his hollowed arena. But custom dictated that all comers would have an equal chance to prove themselves in the Pit. Few laws were observed in Grun, but the laws of the Pit were always upheld and respected. It had been thus since long before Grun existed when the Pit sat alone atop its ancient hill to welcome any seeking fortune and glory.

"And you are aware of the status of this great arena," began the Master tactfully. "It is a hard mistress if you pardon the expression. It grinds through the strongest flesh, even victors are left maimed and wasted. Once you enter, there is no turning back."

"I am aware of the reputation of your Pit," said Lorelei coolly. She expected this attempt at dissuasion and was eager to get it over with.

"If you still wish to fight," said the Pit Master slowly, "then we will begin when you are ready."

Lorelei's green eyes pierced the shadows of her hood like eldritch candles in the darkness. She remained silent and motionless for several long minutes, causing whispers to begin moving through the crowd. Many bets were placed and hushed conversations debated how quickly she would die. Slowly, she reached up and pulled back her hood, keeping her eyes fixed on the Pit Master. Lorelei's hair was pale blonde and cut short so that it hung just past the bottom of her strong sharp jawline. Her bangs were held out of her eyes by a leather headband centered with a green gem. Glittering rings studded her nostrils and both ears. She was lovely and seemed to many nearby, much too young to face this Pit or any other.

"Leave your things here before you enter," said the Master, motioning to the table at his side.

Lorelei's eyes became slits of suspicion and the Pit Master took a step backward as if he received a blow. Such was the sudden power of Lorelei's glare, that sweat ran down his temples and he bit his lip as the tension between them built and became almost too uncomfortable to bear.

The surrounding gamblers grew silent as they waited for this new young fighter to either risk the Pit or turn coward and flee.

"I will guard your things well," said the Master through a dry throat. "You have my word, upon pain of death."

"Very well," nodded Lorelei after another minute of introspection.

The Pit Master sighed and the crowd began to murmur and quickly take bets on the upcoming fight, mostly against the newcomer. Lorelei watched the crowd for a few minutes and then finally she smiled and winked at the Pit Master. She handed him a leather coin-filled pouch. It clinked with some heft in the Master's palm.

"Place a bet for me?" asked Lorelei.

"As you wish," grunted the Master. It was customary for fighters to bet on themselves and the Master was happy to do so, as he always received a cut of the winnings.

With closed eyes, Lorelei whispered to herself, "Oh saga vo Yuggoth se'k maya." Then, she placed on the table her heavy satchel and traveling bag, and her fur-wrapped broadsword. Turning towards the Pit she removed her thick fur-lined cloak, and to the amazement of the gaping throng, she wore no tunic, and her peach skin shined in the light of the surrounding torches. A gruesome tattoo of a human skull without a jaw covered her sternum and smaller skulls connected to it and formed a line that fully encircled the base of her neck, like a grim necklace worn by the damned. She breathed deeply of the night air and a few beads of sweat ran down over the skulls and into the cleft between her bare small breasts. Her torso and limbs were adorned with small scars from past battles, and her stomach was a mass of knotted muscles marked by deep grooves. A wide leather belt pressed against those corded muscles; its surface embedded with gleaming jewels and daggers sheathed on each hip. Except for a pair of worn leather boots, her bottom was as naked as her top. She grinned as the warm night breeze ruffled the hair on her head and the hair between her powerful thighs. Strong arms swung back and forth under thick shoulder muscles as she stretched and prepared for battle. She removed her leather belt and gave it to the Pit Master, and without a word or any fanfare, she jumped into the Pit. She glared up at the whispering, gawking crowd, and the Pit Master knelt and handed her a short-handled single-bladed ax. It was not a subtle weapon, but it suited her fine, as she was not a subtle woman. He retreated and Lorelei swiveled her naked hips and absently ran fingers through her pubic hair as she studied the notches on the sharp, but well-used ax. The scent of blood and sweat laced with adrenaline lingered in the air from the previous fight and spinning the ax in her hand, a thrilling tingle surged through her limbs. She was eager to begin this bloody game.

The Pit Master took his customary position near the tallest of the weathered stone totems and several men and women, minor nobles from the nearby lands, crowded up to his shoulders.

"Never seen a sight like that," said a young handsome nobleman, named Castor. "I'd give her a much more pleasant tumble than what she's about to get in the Pit."

Lorelei glanced up towards the nobles and eyed Castor coolly.

"Oh ho, I think she heard you," said a dark-haired noblewoman named Donetta. She wore a fancy low-cut dress that showed off her ample bosom to its fullest. Her thick lips pouted as she glanced at Lorelei's hard frame and she shrugged. "I bet she gets one look at Brada and comes running into your arms, princeling."

"No," said the balding nobleman Rogerio, who spilled wine prodigiously as he talked. "Not into Castor's puny arms. But I'll give her a good showing, don't you worry, Castor, my boy." Rogerio animatedly tugged on his crotch and spilled more wine onto his dirty boots. "I'll flex for the both of us!" he roared drunkenly.

The other nobles laughed hardily but the Pit Master quickly waved them silent.

"Fools," he said. "This is no harlot or plaything for your amusement. Keep silent if you value your life. She might be a berserker. They fight naked to enhance their rage and lust for battle. I have witnessed a berserker under the influence of the blood-madness, and it was terrible. In those moments, it is best to flee lest you fall under their indiscriminate killing urges. Stay silent and keep your wits."

The nobles looked at the Master quizzically, unsure if he was joking with them.

"Pffha," snorted Rogerio. "What nonsense. Bersherker, shmurzerker."

"We're here to have fun," pouted Donetta playfully as she absently rubbed her hand across Rogerio's groin. "You're too serious, great Pit Master, just because some woman is going to ruin the sport for the evening."

"We shall see," said the Pit Master.

"Well," said Castor as he rubbed his chin, "I bet 20 gold drags against her anyways. She needs more than some perky nipples to win this fight."

The Nobles continued their jesting but Lorelei ignored them and moved her arms to stay loose. She shook her powerful thighs one by one, rolled her shoulders, and stretched her neck. The air was heavy with excitement and she could feel her battle-lust building. The atmosphere in the Pit felt heavy and humid as if it was weighted down by the memories of the violence that it had witnessed over the long years. Sudden claps and howls from the crowd signaled the arrival of Lorelei's opponent, and with a loud thud, his heavy feet landed in the Pit.

"This must be Brada," she thought.

He was a hulking brute with a large beard and a shaved head covered in scars. He wore a vest, boots, and pants all made from wolfskins. His bloodshot eyes glared hungrily at Lorelei and he smiled and licked his lips with a fat purple tongue as he studied her nakedness. He raised his ax high and let out a monstrous bellow. The crowd responded with screams and cheers as their bloodlust surged. Lorelei met his leering eyes with an unwavering steel gaze. After a minute, Brada chuckled, spat at her, and waved his tongue like a panting dog.

The Pit Master let the crowd cheer and yell for a few minutes until he felt their excitement could get no higher, then he struck a small gong. At the sound, Brada charged forward intending to cleave Lorelei's head with one stroke. A quick somersault carried her under and away from Brada's lumbering arm, and as she came to her feet, her ax cut upward through Brada's hamstring, turning his grey pants crimson, and making his ruined leg tremble violently. He spun around and swung his ax in another deadly arc, but Lorelei ducked again and her ax struck deep twice across Brada's stomach. Blood and intestines quickly tumbled towards the pit floor and Brada fell to his knees and tried to hold his guts inside. Lorelei's ax swung again and she laughed as Brada's ax arm fell to the ground, severed at the elbow. Blood sprayed from the waving stump and splashed heavily across Lorelei's naked torso. She paid no attention to the crimson liquid as it ran down her body and through the grooves of her abdominal muscles. Brada moaned in pain, and Lorelei breathed deeply of the iron-scented musk that was clouding around the bleeding man. The crowd was stunned into momentary silence and awe by how quickly this young woman was dismantling the big warrior.

"Unbelievable," whispered Castor to the Pit Master. "Such speed and agility. I have never seen it's like. She moves like a panther."

"Aye," said the Master solemnly.

Brada's low moans became a growl as his pain turned to anger, and he suddenly reached for Lorelei's womanhood, eager to enact some revenge by humiliating this woman in the vilest way possible. But he was much too slow and she caught his wrist before his hand could touch her. With a scowl, her arm muscles bulged and she twisted Brada's wrist until it snapped like dry kindling. Then her ax planted itself into the man's groin, sending a fresh shower of blood onto the stained pit floor, and new exhalations of pain bleated from Brada's strained voice. Lorelei glared at him for a minute as his breathing grew short and fast, and he shivered as he slowly died. She grabbed his beard and tugged his head violently so that he was forced to look into her gleaming emerald eyes.

"You fancy yourself a wolf," she said to him. "But you are just a sheep. And I am a lion."

Lorelei raised her bloody ax high and then slammed it into Brada's neck, sending mighty spouts of fresh blood spraying into the air and onto her naked body. She hacked into her opponent twice more until his head came free. She kicked the wavering corpse to the ground amidst its own gore and she raised the severed head high and glared at the crowd until they began to cheer and howl, like ravenous dogs, eager for more. With a smile, she tossed the gruesome souvenir out of the pit and into the wild howling mass of debauchery.

The Pit Master lowered a ladder and entered the arena cautiously. He handed Lorelei a flagon of beer. Lorelei watched as men with yellow aprons removed Brada's corpse, shoveling his entrails into a sack. She looked at the beer in her mug with suspicion.

"Our best brew, I assure you," said the Pit Master.

"You first," said Lorelei as she handed the mug back to him.

"As you wish," he said before taking a big drink and licking his lips. After a minute he again offered the flagon to Lorelei. "Satisfied?"

Without comment, she quickly downed the entire mug without stopping. Some of the frothing beer spilled down the corner of her mouth and onto her breasts to mix with Brada's blood, but she paid it no heed. When she finished, she tossed the flagon out of the pit towards Castor and the other nobles. Castor caught the mug and smiled at Lorelei. She scowled at him for a moment as Rogerio slapped his back hardily, then she turned back to the Pit Master.

"If you continue, you will face the current Champion," the Master said solemnly. "She has been Champion for five months. She is the best fighter we have seen since I was a young boy. Will you continue?"

"Aye," grunted Lorelei.

"Very well. Do you wish to bet again?"

"If I lose, I can't take it to Valhagga, can I?"

"Very good. I will bet for you. You did well already. Everyone bet on Brada. He was a strong fighter."

"He was a swine," growled Lorelei. "Tell me about this Champion."

"She is a slayer from the far north. Snowland, I think. Bigger than you and savage. Her name is Torgerd. She has killed more than a hundred men in the Pit."

"Snowland, you say? Did she come down the Green-pass, across the great peat bogs to get here, or by the sea route?"

"The bogs, I believe. A dangerous road to tread. What of it?"

"It's nothing," said Lorelei with a wink, but a thought grew quickly in her mind becoming a dangerous plot.

The Pit Master took the ax and handed her a short spear and a long dagger. "Five minutes till the match. I will place your bet." He climbed from the pit.

Lorelei crouched by the wall and ignoring the leering crowd, she urinated. She then stood tall and arched her back into a deep stretch like a panther preparing to hunt. She bounced a bit on her toes, feeling fast and strong, spinning the dagger in her hand, testing its balance. Then, she paced back and forth, full of adrenaline, ready for her next opportunity to spill blood.

The crowd buzzed with energy; bets were placed, ale was drunk, refilled and drunk again, prostitutes were fondled, fights broke out and were quelled, and curses were thrown towards Lorelei by sore losers who had bet heavily on Brada. The next fight promised to be the best they had seen in a long while, and the anticipation made them rabid and wild with excitement. Suddenly, the roar of the crowd erupted, signaling the approach of Torgerd.

Lorelei stopped pacing as the Champion entered the Pit, also armed with a short spear and dagger. Torgerd stood almost a foot taller than Lorelei, and though Lorelei herself had strong thick arms and shoulders, Torgerd's were twice as thick. She had bright orange hair that was pulled away from her face in tight braids that culminated in one long braid that hung down her back past her shoulder blades. She wore a leather sleeveless vest, green pants, and green boots. Her right arm was tattooed with elder runes from the north countries.

Torgerd stepped forward and slowly looked Lorelei up and down, assessing the blood-covered naked woman.

"A wild one, eh?" grunted Torgerd. "You claim to be a daughter of Kurga and Reh, is that it? A disciple of ancient savages, a messenger of the blood gods."

"I claim nothing," responded Lorelei. "I am what I am."

"It takes more to make a berserker than stripping off one's garments," said Torgerd. "Many play at savagery, but the Pit always reveals the truth. You are what you are, huh?"

Torgerd slowly looked Lorelei up and down again, until finally she made up her mind about some matter and nodded to herself. "We shall see," she said.

Lorelei began to pace back and forth, lightly fingering the spear in her hand.

"You come from the Snowland," stated Lorelei. "Have you traveled west of your home, beyond the Black Hills?"

"No," said Torgerd quizzically. "No one has. Not for many a long age. What a strange thing to ask before dying."

"We shall see," cooed Lorelei with a wry smile.

"Ha," smirked Torgerd. "I like you, little savage. You are a riddle. Come on! Forget this crowd of fiends and sycophants. Let's fight and die, for ourselves and no others."

And with that, Torgerd jogged forward, her spear lashing out like a striking snake, followed swiftly by her dagger. Lorelei responded in kind and for a minute they stood in the center of the Pit, parrying and striking, with neither able to gain an upper hand. Then suddenly, Torgerd parried a strike and spun away. Lorelei was caught off balance and stumbled forward. Torgerd's dagger slashed Lorelei's exposed side, her spear slicing across her thigh. Lorelei pulled away and recovered her balance, but once again Torgerd's spear flashed and blood fell from a new wound on Lorelei's chest. The pain focused Lorelei's mind and she launched a fierce counterattack. Torgerd was driven back, a final growl escaped Lorelei's lips as her spear struck deep into Torgerd's side. Torgerd's spear struck back, but Lorelei dodged and her dagger sliced across Torgerd's spear arm, causing her to drop the weapon. Sensing that victory was near, Lorelei pushed forward intending to finish the fiery barbarian, but Torgerd was far from spent. She blocked Lorelei's dagger arm with her own, grabbed Lorelei's opposite armpit, jerked her forward, and delivered a crushing head-butt to Lorelei's face. Blood squirted from Lorelei's nose and her eyes filled with tears. And then Torgerd's knee slammed into Lorelei's groin, and with a violent shove, Lorelei fell with pain wracking her body from head to vulva. Torgerd's heavy boot followed and struck Lorelei in the head leaving her spitting blood on her back trying to remain conscious.

Torgerd took a moment to recover. She snapped the spear shaft that protruded from her side and tossed it away, leaving the rest embedded inside her for the time being.

"I believe there is some berserker in you after all," said Torgerd. "I respect that. I respect your bloodlust, Lorelei, and I will honor it as you die."

Torgerd unbuttoned her leather vest and pulled it off, exposing her heaving breasts which were covered with runes and sunbursts that circled her pink nipples. She stepped towards the crumpled Lorelei and stomped savagely on her stomach. Then, grabbing her by her blond hair, she lifted her onto her knees. Her fist struck downward to pummel Lorelei's face with a force akin to iron striking a log. After two strikes that would have killed a lesser human, Lorelei's inner rage was rekindled. She leapt upward out of Torgerd's grasp and her skull struck Torgerd's jaw, breaking teeth. Her dagger, which she had managed to keep hold of, found purchase in Torgerd's stomach. Torgerd watched with detached fascination as Lorelei's dagger pushed further into her body until the hilt touched her skin. Lorelei growled, looked into Torgerd's eyes, and was met with an icy amused gaze. Then Torgerd's dagger sliced across Lorelei's cheek, followed by another brutal punch that sent Lorelei stumbling back several feet with blood dripping off her face, red spit rolling from her mouth.

The combatants paused and eyed one another dubiously as the crowd hollered and whooped. Lorelei was battered and tired, covered in blood and sweat, but Torgerd had fared worse, though it didn't seem like it. She had a spear point embedded in her side and a dagger hilt deep in her stomach, yet she appeared energized and poised for victory.

"A cruel fate that we had to meet thusly, sister," said Torgerd.

"Aye," said Lorelei. She waved a hand and motioned Torgerd forward. "Our doom awaits."

"Good," exclaimed Torgerd in response as she strode forward with deadly purpose.

The orange-haired barbarian lashed out again and again with her dagger, nearly missing the unarmed Lorelei each time or only scoring small superficial cuts. With a bold lunge, Torgerd struck for the kill, but Lorelei was ready. She caught Torgerd's extended arm with both hands, pinning it against her side. Torgerd moved fast using her free hand to punch Lorelei in the stomach. Here began a brutal stalemate. Each punch delivered by Torgerd against Lorelei's thick core muscles threatened to break ribs and pulp organs, but Lorelei withstood the pounding and refused to release Torgerd's dagger arm, even as blood and spit flew from her mouth with every breath she took. With renewed vigor pulled forth from some deep primal source, Lorelei arched her back, squeezed her arms and Torgerd's extended arm gave way snapping at the elbow. The dagger fell from Torgerd's limp hand. Lorelei released the arm and caught the dagger before it hit the ground. Torgerd's remaining useful hand latched onto Lorelei's throat squeezing it tight. Lorelei's strong neck saved her from a quick death under that vice-like grip. She plunged the dagger upwards under Torgerd's breast, into her heart. Torgerd held Lorelei close and loomed over her. Blood ran heavily from the wound flowing down Lorelei's breasts. Torgerd looked into Lorelei's eyes as she died with a smile on her face. She gently fell to her knees and exhaled one last time.

Torgerd's body slumped further and then fell. Lorelei stepped backward falling to a knee as her injuries overcame her. She knelt for several long minutes staring at Torgerd's corpse until finally standing to be greeted by a wave of rapturous applause and wild cheers. The crowd screamed like hellish fiends, so overjoyed were they at the spectacle they had witnessed.

After regaining some composure, Lorelei climbed a ladder out of the Pit and walked over to the Pit Master. She grabbed a mug of ale from the table and downed it slowly. The nearest people in the crowd gaped at her naked, sweaty, blood-covered flesh. The Pit Master waited patiently for her to finish her drink before bowing his head respectfully.

"A remarkable fight," he said. "Congratulations on your victory, Champion. It will be talked about for years to come."

"I want the body," panted Lorelei, still catching her breath.

"That is unusual," said the Pit Master with raised eyebrows.

"I don't care," she said. "I want a small hand cart, and the body loaded onto it."

"Oi, hold on," said a gruff dirty man nearby. "Custom is we take them bodies. Good money in it for us. Better money than normal for this 'un. We deserve to get ours, same as any other hard-working man."

"That's right," agreed another man with a firm nod. "Listen to Dirk, he'll give ya a good price."

"True," said Dirk. "It's gotta be quick, though, you hear. Her body's still warm, and I got some flamboyant fiends who what wanna have some fun while the gettin's good, know what I mean? We need that body now, so how's about two gold pieces fer it, and you can have it back in an hour. That's fair, it is."

"Good and fair, I say," said the second man.

The Pit Master remained silent as the two men scratched their dirty chins waiting for their generous offer to be accepted. Lorelei scowled and looked down at Torgerd's blood which still glistened on her breasts.

Lorelei slowly lifted her scowl until it met Dirk's eyes. Before he could speak again, Lorelei spun around and grabbed her broadsword from the table. The blade flashed from its scabbard, ripped upward through Dirk's rib cage, and sent blood and gore skyward. Screams and yells of shock flooded the crowd as the downward stroke of Lorelei's sword cleaved its way through the skull of the second man, splitting his face and covering his shirt with a tumbling mass of brains, mucus, and teeth. More men foolishly leapt forward to try and subdue the wild woman. They too fell with spilled innards, severed limbs, and ruptured throats that sprayed blood into the encircling frantic masses.

The nobleman Rogerio was the last to foolishly leap forward. His fine silken shirt was torn asunder by Lorelei's broadsword as his chest was hacked open. He died with a terrible scream. Donetta fell on his spasming body in shock. She pressed her heaving breasts against his face and shook him as if he were just sleeping, wailing as the other nobles backed away, fearing for their own lives.

"You savage slut!" screamed Donetta. "You'll pay for this with your life!"

In response, Lorelei's sword cut through Donetta's slender neck. Her headless corpse fell on top of Rogerio, where it gushed blood like a tipped barrel of wine. Lorelei roared and stabbed the headless body for extra measure. Donetta's blood sprayed the inside of her thighs and when she finally withdrew her sword, Lorelei stood alone in a wide circle filled with butchered bodies and organs steaming in the night air. The crowd was silent and suddenly, gut-wrenchingly, sober.

Castor stepped forward cautiously with outstretched hands. "Calm your anger, please," he begged. "This violence belongs in the Pit, not out of it."

Lorelei's arms shook gently as if she fought with some inner demon, and she raised her sword glaring at Castor like she was looking at him through a dense fog.

"The whole world is a pit," she growled through gritted teeth.

The ferocity in Lorelei's voice was enforced by something darker. It made Castor's veins run cold as he glanced at the Pit Master, whose normally rosy cheeks had turned pale and sweaty.

"Stop now, or I'll have to take you in," offered Castor with fake confidence, trying to establish some authority over the escalating madness. "We forgive much out here, but this slaughter will test even our unscrupulous laws. So, I beg you, lower your sword. The fight is over. You are victorious."

"Take me in?" said Lorelei with a dangerous smile. "You mean, take me for a tumble, don't you?"

Fear filled Castor's eyes as she repeated his own foolish words and like a rabbit suddenly seeing a diving hawk, he turned and fled. He was athletic and fast, but not fast enough, and after running only ten yards, Lorelei's shoulder slammed into his back sending him crashing into a heap. He twitched and grunted in pain, squeezed his eyes tightly and waited for the killing stroke from her sword. But that final blow never fell. After a few seconds, he cautiously opened his eyes to see Lorelei's naked bottom walking away from him, back towards the Pit Master's table and her belongings.

Lorelei knelt and wiped her sword clean on Donetta's fine silk dress, then she sheathed it. She wrapped her heavy cloak about her sweating shoulders and slung her pack across her back.

The Pit Master approached with a shaking hand and offered her a hefty pouch. "Your winnings," he said. "Torgerd's body will be wrapped and placed on a cart for you. It will be unmolested; you have my word."

"Where is the Champion's tent?" she asked.

"At the end of the row," said the Pit Master, pointing a trembling finger. "The black flag with the silver sword. The Champion's squire will draw you a hot bath. Food and drink will be provided, free of charge, of course. And wine."

"No," said Lorelei. "Mead."

"Yes, very good," said the Master with a nod. "You will have mead. The next fights will be in seven days hence..."

"I am leaving tomorrow," interrupted Lorelei, and she turned and left the stunned Pit Master gaping. The crowd gave her a wide berth as she passed them, while many bowed their heads and whispered in awe, 'Champion.'

2. Potions

The sun was just cresting the dew-covered hills, but Lorelei was already pulling her hand cart down the well-trodden dirt road, away from Grun. The slaughter-madness of the previous evening was forgotten in the crisp morning air. She now wore a thin green wool shirt that was buttoned almost to her neck, concealing the skulls that adorned her skin. Though the shirt was fairly loose, her thick shoulders still rippled beneath its folds as she pulled the cart. Her leather, jewel-studded belt pressed against her dark blue pants and she no longer wore her headband, preferring to let her blonde hair blow in the morning breeze.

A lone figure with a wide-brimmed hat pulled low followed behind her at a good sixty yards. Lorelei was pretty sure she knew who it was, but she wasn't going to stop her journey to speak with them. If they caught up to her, so be it. She had pressing business elsewhere.

After pulling the cart for another twenty minutes Lorelei stopped in front of a lonely stone cottage. No other buildings were within sight. The cottage had a large garden surrounding it, which in turn, was surrounded by a short stone wall. A wooden sign near the road declared that this was the location of an Herbalist. Lorelei walked into the garden space which was heaving with bees and butterflies, gave a quick knock, and entered the cottage. Inside, the space was packed with tables and with shelves that covered all the walls up to the ceilings. On everything there were jars, wicker baskets and wooden bowls laden with plants, herbs, poultices, and powders. A young boy stood behind the only table with an uncluttered top. He straightened his apron and bowed his head.

"Good day, My Lady," he said. "May I help you?"

Lorelei walked further into the shop and glanced about. When she finally came to rest in front of the boy her emerald eyes studied him sharply and he gasped.

"Ch-champion," he stuttered softly. He bowed again, even lower. "Wh-what can I get you, Champion? I am at your service."

"I am looking for something very particular," began Lorelei as her eyes scanned the shelves. "Something rare."

Her gaze locked onto a dusty jar on a shelf in a corner of the shop that no light seemed to penetrate. She smiled with relief and pointed at the jar. "That is what I am after," she said. "The black roots of Nergul."

The boy shuddered and he glanced at the jar with fear. "I am sorry, Champion, but that is not for sale. It is a ghastly trophy, owned by the Master Herbalist, nothing more. Perhaps I can get you some…"

"No," she interrupted firmly but gently. "I need the roots."

"B-but," he stammered, "my Master is not here. I couldn't sell those without his leave."

Lorelei's hands rested on her hips, near the handles of her daggers.

The boy looked at the weapons and cringed, beads of sweat formed on his young brow. Lorelei's hand moved and the boy flinched, but instead of grabbing a dagger, it pulled forth a sizable coin purse. The boy sighed deeply as Lorelei pulled out a handful of gold drags which she stacked on the tabletop. The boy gaped at the sight of so much money and remained frozen until Lorelei's voice brought him back into the moment.

"Grab the jar," she said softly. "Your Master will understand."

Reluctantly, the boy did as he was told, carrying the dusty jar with its thick smoky glass at arms-length, petrified by its contents. He placed the jar on the table, lifted the lid, and immediately a decrepit odor wafted into the air. The light in the shop wavered. The boy took a step backward, but Lorelei leaned in close to examine the contents.

"I c-can't touch that," whimpered the boy.

"I will handle it," said Lorelei. She pulled out a thick scrap of cloth which she used to grab the large black roots. She wrapped them up and put them in a pouch which she tied shut firmly. The light increased as soon as the roots were out of sight and the sweet aromas of the herbs spread through the air once again.

The boy breathed heavily as if he had just escaped some doom and that is when he was startled anew by another person entering the cottage. The newcomer had a wide-brimmed hat pulled low. They motioned to the door.

"Leave, boy," said a man's commanding voice.

The boy glanced at Lorelei then back to the newcomer. He grabbed the pile of gold coins and left quickly. Lorelei kept her back to the stranger, her hands gently tapping the pommels of her daggers. A smile began to spread across her lips. The man stayed close to the door. After a minute of silence, he removed his hat and ran a hand through his shaggy hair.

"So, Castor," said Lorelei without turning around, "our paths cross again. What a coincidence that we are traveling in the same direction."

"Not really," began Castor, cautiously. "I followed you."

"I know," laughed Lorelei. The sound of that laughter was light and full of joy, stunning Castor. "You would make a terrible spy or brigand," she continued. "Why do you follow me, nobleman?"

"I-I don't know," he said honestly.

"Have you come for revenge," she hissed.

"No," exclaimed Castor quickly. "I just needed to see you again, one last time. That's all."

Lorelei turned to face him and her quick movement made Castor jump back. He knocked over some jars on a table as his back smacked against it. He cringed at his clumsiness and silently cursed. Lorelei smiled, thinking he looked like a startled doe frozen with uncertainty. He looked at her, cleared his throat, but didn't speak.

Lorelei giggled, "Do I scare you?"

"A little," said Castor reluctantly.

"You need not fear me," smiled Lorelei. "I won't hurt you. You believe me, don't you?"

"Mord, the Pit Master, said you come from the Blue Isle," ventured Castor, not responding to her question. "I have never heard of such a place. Are all its peoples like you?"

"You mean, are they bloody-handed barbarians?" Lorelei smirked playfully.

"N-no," stammered Castor. "That's not what I meant, well, I meant that, well, you see..."

"Calm yourself," said Lorelei with open hands as if Castor was a skittish horse she needed to soothe. "My homeland is a small island far from here. Its people are peaceful farmers that spend their days among beautiful pastures and slopping flower-covered hills. It is a paradise."

Castor's brow creased with puzzlement. How could such a savage woman come from such a perfect land? He silently studied Lorelei's bruised yet still beautiful face, desiring that one moment in her presence to last forever.

"I have far to go and time is of the essence," said Lorelei, breaking the silence. "You needed to see me again, and you have. So, Castor, my young noble, have you seen everything you wanted to see?"

"I don't really know," said Castor with a roguish smile as he looked at the floor. "It was a foolish compulsion, and I apologize. I will leave you to your business."

"I am not a violent lover," she said softly as her eyes sparkled. Castor's head jerked up at the statement, giving Lorelei, the exact reaction she desired. She licked her smiling lips.

"I actually prefer men that are much less savage than I. Does that surprise you, Castor? I think it does."

Lorelei kicked off her boots, her fingers unbuttoned her wool shirt as she slowly moved towards Castor. His eyes grew large as he first saw the grim tattoo of the skull necklace followed by hard muscles then small beautiful breasts as Lorelei's shirt was gently tossed to the floor.

"You take many lovers, yes?" she asked rhetorically. "Every week perhaps, while the Pit churns through flesh like a murderous mill, grinding bodies with steel for your pleasure. After the blood is spent you ravage some soft debutante or pampered harlot. That must grow dull and tiresome."

Lorelei let her wide jeweled belt drop to the floor, followed swiftly by her pants, which she stepped out of as she came face-to-face with Castor. They were the same height and the nobleman was stunned as he stared into the depths of her emerald eyes. His heartbeat was like a pounding war drum in his ears. Her powerful naked body hovered inches away intimidating him but also exciting him. He felt the heat of her body. She smelled like rosemary and mint. The scent was intoxicating. His body trembled and he felt the surge of lust in his loins.

"I take few lovers," she said. "I've taken none for many months. It is too long a time for such a basic need. Such a primitive need."

Her hands worked gently to unclasp Castor's belt and tug down his breeches. "I am not soft like the women of Grun," she said as she placed his trembling hands upon her muscular hips. She raised her left leg setting her foot on a shelf by Castor's knee, aligning her moist entrance to his manhood.

"Will you have me, son of nobles?" she asked softly.

Her hands stroked his firm erection and with a guttural moan she pulled him inside of her until he could go no further. He whispered, "Yes," before they kissed passionately and began their heated dalliance.

The afternoon sun shone down through dappled clouds as Lorelei pulled her hand cart down the seldom-used Green-pass, miles from the village of Grun. There were no houses or farmsteads this far north of the village, and her only companions were the wild animals she crossed; foxes, birds, deer, badger, and rabbits. It was good to get away from the grime and decay of

Grun, thought Lorelei as she paused to rest. Her mind briefly thought of Castor, whom she had left panting and exhausted in the herbalist's hut a mere two hours ago. She smiled, laughed to herself, and gave a silent prayer to her Gods that Castor would remain well and unharmed for many years.

She looked about studying the small standing stones that now dotted the landscape. They had been erected so long ago that no tales could tell who had put them there, and their appearance told her she was getting very close to her destination. The wider Grun territory ended on its north edge at a great expanse of deadly peat bogs, the border of which was marked by a long row of thin stones standing seven feet high. She could see those stones in the near distance, like fence-posts placed by giants. In front of that row of posts and slightly off to her right was an even more impressive and esoteric sight; a massive double circle of cyclopean rocks standing twenty feet high with lintels across their tops like doorways to the past. Lorelei wiped some sweat from her brow, shook out her shoulders and pulled her cart towards the stone circles.

The closer she got, the larger the stones became, until they towered over her with their impressive weight and bearing. Crows perched on the outer ring of stones, but would not fly over the monumental circle. They were careful to fly around the perimeter. Lorelei could feel an aura emanating from the spaces beyond the rocks, yet nothing strange was visible. Standing in the shadow of one stone she studied the layout of the site. The large monolithic rocks stood on end in a wide, flat-topped circle that pointed to the stars as if it were a beacon for cosmic beings that wished to enter the world. Inside this ancient ring a smaller ring of stones formed a tighter circle around a flat stone in the center acting like an altar or stage, ready and willing to host unnamed rituals, no matter how obscene or abhorrent. Nothing else could be seen within the stones and after several additional minutes of silent study, Lorelei was satisfied.

In the nearby meadows, across the vast peat bog she could hear innumerable birds chirping and singing and insects buzzing. Lorelei sat in the shade of one great stone, rested, ate a small meal, and waited for nightfall. When the last rays of the sun fell behind the distant hills, Lorelei stood up, readied herself, and grabbed her cart.

Entering the big ring of stones was like entering another world and Lorelei immediately felt the air grow warmer and more humid. The sounds of nature in the surrounding fields and bog disappeared, as an unknown force made her legs feel heavier with each step as if it was giving her time to reconsider and turn back. Her heartbeat increased as she pushed on, pulling her cart behind her. Upon entering the smaller stone circle, the humidity grew even thicker. Sweat began to roll down her temples and neck. She could feel it run down her chest, over her gruesome tattoo, down between her breasts and beyond. A hot unnatural wind blew around the inner circle and Lorelei noticed several large serpents move through the grass away from her as she approached the altar. She looked up to see a night sky that somehow shined more brilliantly than it did outside the circle. Forms, vague yet sinister, crossed the stars with their dark shimmering shapes and a creeping madness pressed itself upon her. Despite the hot air, a chill ran down her spine and her knees momentarily grew weak. She shook her head, grunted, and pushed away the fatigue and warning in her mind. This strange location was perfect for her needs.

Lorelei lifted Torgerd's body from the cart and laid it flat on the altar. She unwrapped it carefully, and gently ran her fingers over the runic tattoos that covered Torgerd's cold breasts.

"Forgive me, sister," she said. "I know not what Gods you favor, or were favored by, but I bring you to this place of power that is undoubtedly older than those beings. You will be outside their grace and I am sorry."

Leaving the body on the cold stone she knelt in the grass pulling several items from her pack, including a deep bowl, bags of herbs, a small book, the curling black root from the herbalist, and her broadsword. With a dagger, she dug a hole in the moist earth. As she dug, she could feel the ground shudder and ripple in either pain or pleasure. A powerful aroma surged forth from the dirt sending small shock-waves of adrenaline and lust through her body. The musk of the ancient earth coursed through her veins as she dug faster, eager to complete her business in this eldritch and inhuman space. Into the hole she tossed several herbs and plants, and the odorous black root of Nergul. She cut a line across her hand letting her blood drip into the hole until the root was covered. The ground shuddered again as the black root quickly absorbed the blood and began to twitch in pleasure. She filled the hole back in with dirt, opened the small book, and began to read. As she did, her voice sunk lower and lower until it boomed with a deep unearthly resonance.

Her lips quivered, her heart pounded, and sweat poured down her temples and her body. The incantation lasted for many long minutes and her eyes sparkled as they strained against the eldritch words. The brightness of the stars overhead illuminated the space with an eerie light. A strange fog began to rise from the ground in select spots where it would meet the hot circling air creating spinning vapors that reflected the starlight. With a jolt, as if she had been struck, Lorelei released the book and leaned forward, exhausted. The air became still in anticipation and Lorelei remained motionless for fear of breaking her necromancy. The loose dirt began to stir. At first, it looked like a root was pushing up out of the earth, but as it grew it glistened like a worm. It was followed by other tentacles until a small body emerged, to which the tentacles were all attached. The horrific creature crawled into the grass as several more emerged from the hole to follow the first. Lorelei gazed at them with a mix of wonder, terror, and satisfaction, as they pawed at her legs.

Suddenly, a deep and unearthly hoot, like an owl, but filled with malice and a hellish hunger, reverberated through the stone circle. Lorelei backed away from the flopping tentacled creatures, grabbing her broadsword just as a demonic shape fell out of the black sky on fluttering flesh-covered wings. The sight of the creature nearly made her retch, such was the overpowering madness of its slug-like body and writhing tentacled arms. Stars that were not of this world glittered across its reflective mucus-covered skin. With an extended, fang-encrusted orifice, its eyeless head bent down to devour the small creatures which Lorelei had just birthed from the soil.

She fought back a surge of panic that would have sent other people running and screaming. With a growl that steadied her limbs, she lunged forward to hack at the creature with murderous blows. The demon spasmed and rolled as Lorelei's sword cut great gashes into its blubbery hide. Its purple blood flowed into the grass shimmering and steaming like hot cosmic oil. Lorelei pressed her attack and chunks of abhorrent flesh fell away amidst clumping, writhing gore, but the monster would not die. Suddenly, it launched a counterattack. Its snapping mouth appendage fought against her steel blade and she was hard pressed to keep its fangs from clamping onto her neck. Its tentacled legs lashed about her body in crushing, grasping waves, and she was nearly overpowered by the weight of the beast. The tentacles circled her waist, chest, and her thighs, and they tore at her clothes, searching for flesh that they could rend and abuse. The fetid stench of this elder nightmare sought to choke her and break her mind. Mucus was flung from its body towards her mouth where the taste of it caused her to vomit repeatedly, even as she fought against its bulk. Smaller, stinging tentacles slapped her neck and the pain nearly broke her. She could feel her arms going numb and weakening. The beast pushed forward and her body was struck over and over with tentacles that hit like hammers. She clenched her muscles to withstand the beating while small goo-covered tongues wrapped around her hands and her sword so that she couldn't use them.

Her legs and arms shook violently, her muscles strained against the assault, but it was to no avail. She knew that any minute now her body would give out and she would be torn apart and consumed by the demon.

With a vile shriek, the tentacles of the beast ripped through her pants and pressed against her groin as more tore through her shirt and grasp her breasts. In that final moment when all seemed lost, a battle-madness born of revulsion and the primal desire for survival overtook her. With a roar, she ripped her arms free from the lashing tongues, and in two strokes she severed the biting mouth, then stabbed deeply into what she assumed was the thing's head. The tentacles began to release as the monster slowed its assault and shuddered. Lorelei pressed on with more furious blows until the front of the beast completely fell away from the rest of the horrific body. She stumbled backward, panting as the purple star-glistening form slowly stopped twitching. She gave pause for only a moment, then busied herself with an even more gruesome task. With her dagger and her strong arms, she butchered and dissected the corpse until she found a large organ that glowed pale with an eerie luminescence. Somehow, it still trembled with abhorrent life.

"Thank you, Lord Reh," she whispered with genuine awe and reverence.

She quickly placed the beating organ in her bowl, and with the pommel of her sword, she began to mash it up. It released a terrible squeal which quickly faded into the night as its mass turned into a jelly that glowed brightly with green iridescence. Lorelei took the bowl and knelt by Torgerd's body. She gave pause considering what she was about to do. The hot wind sprung up again fiercely and Lorelei's blond hair whipped about. On that wind she heard the whispers of necromancers and wizards, and her skin shivered as if suddenly cold. She shook her head, glaring at the dark clouds blowing wildly overhead, then she smeared the jelly heavily onto Torgerd's most gruesome wounds. The jelly bubbled and smoked as it touched Torgerd's flesh.

Lorelei dumped some mead from a flask into the bowl to dissolve the rest of the jelly into a drinkable form. She carefully poured some of the liquid down Torgerd's throat, then with a silent curse, she drank the rest herself. Instantly, she could feel the liquid stretch out and spread through her body. Her muscles flexed without her bidding, her breathing became heavy, a purple vapor spilled from her mouth and tears ran down her cheeks as she clutched at her pounding chest. Her breathing relaxed, and she smiled as she felt her wounds knitting themselves together.

After several minutes, the throbbing sensations grew, deepened, and rippled through her body. An uncontrollable joyous quivering overtook her and she grunted and cursed as she orgasmed long and hard. The throbbing slowly subsided after a second orgasm and new vigor coursed through her limbs and her mind. She studied Torgerd's body and saw that a similar range of spasms and flexions were moving through her. Torgerd stopped moving and remained still, and Lorelei held her breath until Torgerd's tattooed chest began to rise and fall in a steady rhythm.

After another few minutes, Torgerd's eyes fluttered open. She turned her head and looked at Lorelei. "The berserker," she said softly.

"Yes, sister," said Lorelei with a smile. "Welcome back."

Torgerd sat up and she felt for the death wound under her breast, but it was gone and only a small scar remained. It was the same for the wounds on her stomach and side. She flexed her arms, shook her legs, then turned back to Lorelei.

"I am alive? How is this possible? I know that I died in the Pit." She smiled broadly. "Glorious was our battle. Oh, how I relished it."

"You are resurrected," whispered Lorelei. "Forgive me, if that troubles you."

Torgerd thought silently for a minute, looked about, and she studied Lorelei's torn clothes with their glistening purple stains. Her eyes fell upon the butchered shimmering mass of the demon. Goose bumps rippled across her strong arms. With an effort she pulled her gaze from its corpse and looked at Lorelei.

"Are you a sorceress as well as a slayer?" she asked. "What has befallen thee?"

"With the blessing of Lord Reh, I called upon nameless Elder Beings from beyond time to aid me. A great child of Yuggoth came, and I was nearly overcome, but Reh gave me strength and I prevailed. The essence of that cosmic horror healed you, and me. I am no sorceress and damned lucky to be alive. Does that answer suit you?"

"Dark necromancy," mumbled Torgerd. A cold shiver ran up and down her spine as she thought about this answer for several minutes before finally nodding.

"And why did you resurrect me, berserker? Do you wish to fight again? Another glorious battle with only the Gods as witnesses."

"One fight with you was more than enough," smiled Lorelei. "I saved you from defilement and dishonor so that you might aid me in a perilous adventure."

"Perilous?" Torgerd's eyes sparkled. "What aid do you ask of me?"

"I need your help to cross the peat bogs yonder. And then, we go west and cross the Black Hills."

"Ha," said Torgerd as she pulled in her legs and crossed them. "You are truly mad, young savage. No one crosses the Black Hills. It is the realm of foul sprites and forest demons. It is no place for humans, and it will reward our trespassing with violent torture and death. Let's go back to Grun and bargain with the Pit Master. We can grow fat on the wealth that the Pit offers. Two Champions could bring that arena of slaughter glory beyond its reckoning."

"No," said Lorelei with a gentle shake of her head. "I seek treasures far greater than what Grun could provide in a hundred lifetimes."

"There is no such treasure in the world of the living," snorted Torgerd. "Unless you wish to go East and topple entire kingdoms. But two fighters, though mighty we be, are not an army."

Lorelei leaned in close, her eyes sparkling in the starlight. "Deep in the Black Hills there is a great valley, and at the center stands a black temple that was ancient when men first stood on two legs. This temple is home to Kaigora, the Serpent Queen, eldest of all the fair folk. Born to the first elves at the dawn of the world, her hunger for knowledge and wealth changed her into something great and terrible. It is rumored among the dark priests of Jutt, that she fucks and devours her followers in a vast chamber filled with the jewels of the Earth. It is wealth enough to blast the mind, but even the Ancient Gods, themselves greedy for treasure, will not dare to enter the temple, such is the terror and power of Kaigora."

Torgerd was silent for a long while and naught could be heard but the evening songs of crickets and toads. Finally, she nodded her head.

"You speak of a demonic elvish realm and a ruthless demi-god. Can your savagery overcome such a thing? This is a test that may leave us broken and wasted, even if we are victorious. There is no guarantee we can even win through the Black Hills to reach this orgy of madness. Do you truly wish to find the temple of dread, and face the Serpent Queen?"

"Aye," said Lorelei, and her eyes sparkled mischievously.

"Then I will go with you, Lorelei, and may Bodrum and Odindisa protect our souls. I am indebted to you and my life remains in your hands till that debt is settled. We will go to the Black Hills and we will fight, and die if we must, for each other and no one else."

"Tonight, we rest," said Lorelei, "and tomorrow we head north towards fortune or ruin."

3. Dogs

Death Bog it was called, and crossing its nondescript soft peat surface was a slow business. The spongy ground was formed by layers of moss, centuries old, and its instability could quickly trap living things and suck them down into the depths where they would suffocate. It formed a natural wall between the far northern realms and the vast tribal lands west of the Triple Rivers, and it was nearly impassable. Torgerd, however, had crossed it once before, and she explained to Lorelei that plants grew differently if they were on the peat as opposed to firmer ground. The width of the grass blades, the color and shape of the clover, the height of the dandelions and the iridescence on the backs of beetles; all these factors could tell Torgerd if they were safe or in danger of stepping into the moist peat. To Lorelei, everything looked the same, and she knew that without Torgerd's guidance she would die in the bog, sucked under to suffocate gruesomely like thousands before her.

Whenever Torgerd became unsure, which wasn't often, she used a long walking stick to prod the turf and determine the safest route. All the ground felt the same to Lorelei, and once, out of curiosity, she stepped onto what she deemed to be safe ground, and her foot quickly sank to her knee. It was difficult to recover her leg from the clinging peat, even with her great strength. She watched Torgerd closely after that with a greater appreciation for her woodlore, and with a more acute fear of the Death Bog. She wanted to scream and run and be away from it, but she could not. To counter the madness of her instincts, she breathed deeply and slowly and turned her mind to other things.

They had abandoned Lorelei's hand cart before traversing the bog, and instead, Torgerd carried her own traveling pack, which Lorelei had acquired for her before leaving Grun. It was filled with food and provisions, and everything a traveler might need on a long journey. Lorelei had also supplied Torgerd with weapons; several daggers, a broadsword, and a double-bladed battle axe. Torgerd wore a dark red shirt with a smattering of embroidered blue flowers along with her standard green pants and boots.

Lorelei had switched to a blue shirt that she only loosely buttoned, and short pants made from soft and flexible leather. She had burned the torn and blood-soaked clothes from the previous day, along with the ancient demon's body. Phantoms drifted and swirled in the smoke and reek of that burning corpse, and afterward, the ground was scarred bright blue for many years. Wandering druids and pilgrims seeking ancient guidance would come to those circles, but abandon them quickly when they saw the glittering signs of the arcane slaughter.

Walking the bog was tedious and dull, and to pass the time Torgerd would sing softly in her northern tongue, or Lorelei would tell tales of adventures she survived in the great dungeon catacombs of the Ulbrik Wizards, or her fights against vampires in the city of Herdleberg, or of her time as a scout in the Warband of the Mercenary King, Comus. Torgerd would listen to these bloody and arresting tales silently, and only occasionally would she ask questions, and the answers would make her chuckle. Lorelei detailed men and women she had seduced and then robbed, how she split people apart in battles or drunken arguments, the lusty sex she had in broad daylight, devious things she did with the decapitated heads of her enemies, and horrific demons she had witnessed in dark forbidden places. And in this way, the companions spent three days slowly moving across the great Death Bog, sweating in the humid air by day, and drinking mead by a rousing fire of peat by night.

On the morning of the fourth day, Torgerd threw down her walking stick and exclaimed, "We are free, Lorelei. We have survived the deadly peat and left it behind. Welcome to the borders of the north country."

"I'm tired of this slow trudge," said Lorelei and she shook her mighty thighs one at a time. "Let's jog awhile. We have treasure to find and demi-gods to slay, and not a moment to spare."

"Agreed," said Torgerd heartily. And with that, they started at a nice easy pace, jogging to the west, and the miles fell away and their pounding lungs felt good.

It wasn't long before the land began to rise and fall, and small hillocks filled the landscape like an endless cemetery of barrows. And after jogging through the small hills for several miles, the clover on the ground became dark purple and this made the land seem otherworldly. Small pink flowers grew on the very tops of the hills but did not touch the sides or the valleys between.

"The Black Hills," grumbled Torgerd as she pulled some of the dark clovers and studied them.

"Aye," smirked Lorelei. "Not too black, is it?"

They made camp and lit no fire, and the next day took them further west into the Black Hills. As the day wore on, tension arose in the air and grew steadily until it was palpable and unsettling. A miasma of dread filled the spaces between the hills and short sharp thistles appeared among the clover and heather, adding to the menace of the landscape. Shapes could be seen from the corners of their eyes, darting from view around the hills. They thought it to be foxes or birds at first, but they slowly realized that some higher intelligence was stalking them and they could feel the danger and malice in the slinking shadows. Dusk was approaching fast and the companions continued westward, but the darting shapes kept their dogged pursuit.

Lorelei grew tired of this shadow game and was ready to chase after the dark shapes until a sudden blood-curdling howl cut through the tense air. Several other howls answered from all around the hills and the hair on Lorelei's neck bristled and her scalp crawled at the eerie sounds. Wolf-like it was, but fiercer and fouler, and imbued with unwholesome intent. She pressed her back against Torgerd's and she drew her sword. The howls continued and were like ice in their veins and Torgerd thumbed the handle of her axe nervously.

"Werewolves," said Torgerd softly.

That bestial name was a dagger of fear that pressed itself into Lorelei's bosom. Her flesh crawled and her eyes darted to and fro, searching for the dog-faced demons. And from the cleft between two hillocks came a small figure, dwarfish in height, with a black beard and a naked body covered in blue tattoos. He walked forward a few paces and then glared at the warrior women with eyes that blazed with red light, like coals in a fire.

"You are not welcome here, humans," he said with a deep voice. "You have strayed from your world and must face the consequence of your trespass."

"We have not strayed," barked Lorelei defiantly. "We are exactly where we planned to be. Let us pass or you will meet sharp steel guided by slaying arms."

"You have spirit, yellow hair," growled the dwarf. "And strong hips, too. We require both. Your days of slaying with steel are over, foolish human rabbits. We usually range far to hunt, and it is rare that game comes so readily into our land. The Black Hills are our domain, and our cauldrons will boil this night, stuffed with your bones, if you do not submit to us!"

"Come closer, fiend," spat Torgerd as she hefted her axe high. "I'll show you how we submit to filthy dogs."

The dwarf began to laugh, and as he did, his body began to change. His thighs expanded and lengthened, and his skin moved like wet clay. His torso popped and creaked, his ribs shifted about and his quaking chest stretched wide. His shoulders shook violently and ballooned in thickness, his arms flailed about as they grew hideously long, and his fingers stretched and bled as long heavy claws burst from his fingertips. He coughed up thick saliva and shook his head as his neck stretched, popped, and expanded. His genitals ejaculated repeatedly as they thickened and strained, and he grunted violently and shat in the heather. He opened his mouth wide as his canines grew into large fangs and his face distorted and stretched forward gruesomely until it resembled a wolf with large black ears. Shaggy black fur sprouted to cover his arms, head, chest, and groin, and where his naked flesh was still visible it darkened in color. In a matter of a few horrific moments, the dwarf had been replaced by a great black werewolf, standing tall on freakish legs with extra-long arms that hung below his knees and a great fang-filled muzzle that snarled in front of red eyes. He shook his head and his long ears flapped. Then he pointed his head to the darkening sky and howled with such abhorrent force that Lorelei flinched.

In response to that howl, shapes began to appear from the hills, surrounding the women. They stalked forward, some on two legs, some on four, a great pack of werewolves eager to feast and play with gouged human flesh. The hellish dogs were either brown or gray and white, with burning yellow eyes. The black-furred leader gave a harsh bark and the attack began.

"Don't let them bite you," warned Torgerd. "Their saliva will change you into one of them if you are not killed outright."

The werewolves charged forward with reckless abandon, and the fastest wolf was the first to die. Torgerd's axe split its head in half. She bellowed like a mad bull and leapt forward into the fray. Her axe danced about turning the dark clover red and sending blood spurting into the air. While one wolf died under her powerful strokes, another would cut her with its claws until it too felt the slaughtering bite of her axe. This sequence continued for wolf after wolf, and Torgerd ignored her growing expanse of wounds as she hacked and slew.

Lorelei was also hard pressed by wolves, as they darted here and there, and goaded her with yips and growls. Their taunting hideous faces enraged her. When one grey wolf finally got too close, she lunged and her sword cut halfway through its long neck. The wolf flopped and thrashed but its blood gushed heavily from the wound. Its fellows ignored its pain and stepped on the dying dog as they leapt towards Lorelei. With a roar, she stabbed her sword through the eye socket of a mangy tan wolf as it sought to bite her. It kicked and tugged for a second with blood oozing from its mouth before it died, and Lorelei's corded muscles fought to keep hold of her sword. She managed to pull her steel free just as another wolf pounced, and the arc of her blade cut open its abdomen spilling bright entrails. The wolf trampled and tore its own intestines as it scrambled in the clover, but it didn't die. It attacked again.

The wolf's stinking body slammed into Lorelei and her sword was knocked from her hand even as it cleaved through the wolf's shoulder. It clawed at her fiercely and more of its organs fell from the great gash in its body, and she felt the heat of them as they rolled down her thighs. She clamped a hand onto its muzzle to keep its fangs from sinking into her flesh, swiftly drew one of her daggers and began to stab repeatedly into the beast's thick neck. The third and fourth stabs cut open a great chunk of the hairy neck, blood gushed from the wound and the wolf twitched violently. Then with a final shudder, it went limp.

Lorelei shoved the butchered body into the heather and frantically looked about for her sword. Just then, a noose was looped over her head and as her dagger ripped into the heart of another charging wolf, the rope of the noose was violently yanked tight. Lorelei dropped her dagger and pulled at the noose— fear of a slow choking death flooded her mind. A red-haired wolf with matted oily fur leapt forward and tossed a handful of glittering powder into Lorelei's face. She inhaled the dust and began to drool, the world around her began to spin and grow fuzzy. The wolf barked and struck her with its large fists. She was helpless to defend herself from the barrage as her hands were busy trying to hold the noose at bay. A final great swing from the beast sent Lorelei to the ground in a bloody daze.

Just then, Torgerd came to her aid with a banshee scream, and her axe sheared off the red wolf's arm. The severed appendage sprayed blood across Torgerd's thighs, as she struck again and cut through the wolf's ribs, into its heart. It spasmed and flopped for a moment as Torgerd ripped her axe free, but she was then overcome by two more werewolves that leapt upon her back and bore her to the ground. The three combatants rolled in the clover and fought. The wolves clawed at Torgerd cutting gouges in her flesh, but she kept their jaws at bay. She abandoned her axe and drew a long dagger, sticking it into a wolf throat. It kicked at her and clawed her arms, but with a murderous tug, she pulled the dagger from one fur-covered ear to the other. The second wolf lunged with its jaws wide, ready to tear and rend, but Torgerd was faster. She dodged the fangs and plunged her dagger through the wolf's skull into its vile brain.

With a pile of bleeding corpses at her feet, Torgerd regained her axe and spun it about, laughing with grim satisfaction. Her wounds were too numerous to count, and though they bled down her arms, chest and back, none were deep enough to truly maim her. Five great werewolves remained, plus their black-furred leader. Four of these circled Torgerd, while the fifth, a white wolf, tugged hard on the rope around the neck of Lorelei who moaned and rolled in the blood-soaked clover.

"I will never become a flea-infested demon like you," laughed Torgerd. "My forebears split wolves like kindling, and so do I. I'll cut my own throat before I become a dog in your pack of bastards."

"So be it," growled the black wolf. "We have gained one convert this night, we do not need two, though the pack is short of mothers. You weaken with every second as your blood leaks from your body. Soon, we will tear you apart and consume you, barbarian. You have slain many, but you have lost."

Torgerd snarled as her spinning axe kept the wolves at bay, but she knew the leader was right. She could already feel her energy draining as her wounds continued to drip with every breath she took. Time was against her. She could almost feel the icy north wind on her face, could hear the crashing of waves against the shore and the songs of the druids over the great barrows. Torgerd laughed to herself and plotted her final moves. She kept her last dagger close and thought about how she wished to die.

Nearby, Lorelei's body was completely numb. Her arms and legs would not respond to her foggy mind as she drooled and coughed and cried. Her vision went dark as she keeled over into the clover and thistles, she mumbled incoherently and her powerful frame shivered uncontrollably. As consciousness slowly left her, fear clawed at her mind and she whispered a final prayer to her Gods.

4. Sisters

White wispy clouds moved lazily across a blue sky, and a cool breeze stroked short meadow grasses dotted with yellow dandelions and purple blazing stars. Small goats frolicked about, butted heads, and nibbled on the greenery, and two girls lounged about watching them and enjoying the day. The eldest was nineteen and she was tall and lean and beautiful, and her auburn hair was pulled into a tight braid. The younger girl was fourteen and her blond hair was left wild and free, and it chaotically framed her face as she rolled in the grass and stared at the clouds. She was shorter than the older girl, but someday she hoped to be just as tall and just as beautiful. She wore a white short-sleeve top and red pants that ended above her boney knees.

"Can we skip the festival tonight and stay out here?" asked the young girl while she chewed on a long grass stem.

"No, Lorelei," said the older girl. "Mother would be disappointed. Besides, she made you a new dress, and she wants to see you wear it."

"Oh, yeah," said Lorelei with a hint of disappointment.

"Plus, there will be dancing and lots of cute boys."

"Aww, Gwen," snorted Lorelei, "I don't want to dance with any boys."

Gwen laughed at her sister. "Well, I do," she said. Then she stood up and stretched her tall frame. She wore long pants and tall boots that made her look even taller than she was. She kicked Lorelei in the leg. "Come on, Lor. Let's get the herd moving towards home."

"Ugh," sighed Lorelei, and she begrudgingly pulled herself to her feet.

"So dramatic," laughed Gwen, and she ran her fingers through Lorelei's mess of hair. "I think I saw one of the new grey fawns going into the ravine down by the hedgerow. Go and find him, will you? I'll round up the others."

"Okay," said Lorelei, and she set off at a jog. "I'll see you at home!"

"Aye," said Gwen, and she turned away and walked towards the goat herd.

Lorelei jogged and skipped through the meadow, her wiry frame bouncing with energy. The small ravine had been formed over the years by water running off the fields, and it was shaded by a neat row of apple trees and hedges. Lorelei could see a mess of goat prints in the soft dry dirt, but she couldn't tell if any were recent, so she continued and followed the ravine for several miles, but never saw the grey goat. She began to daydream about pirates and dragons as she walked, and after more than an hour, she paused to get her bearings.

"Maybe Gwen was wrong," she mumbled to herself. "He wouldn't have gone this far by himself. Nobody ever comes out here, not even goats."

Just then an eagle screeched and flew over her head, and Lorelei watched it closely as it disappeared over a large lonely hill. After a minute, Lorelei finally recognized where she was, and a rush of excitement and fear coursed through her. The hill was a forbidden place known as Horgun's Hill. It was named after an ancient giant by the first settlers of the Blue Isle, but it had no real connection to Horgun, as far as Lorelei knew. It was a cursed and haunted place, according to legends, and it was rare that anyone even ventured within sight of the great mound. Lorelei knew that if one of her sisters were here, they would have yanked her arm and quickly turned back. But Lorelei was different from her sisters. She was more curious and adventurous and less superstitious. Suddenly, she thought about the waves crashing on the rocks near her home, and how they attacked with ferocious abandon, but the hard rocks stood firm and defiant and protected the island from the sea. That idea made her feel good, and it bolstered her courage, and she began to climb the hill. Her excitement grew with each step she took, and slowly, her legs propelled her higher and higher up the grassy knoll, and the warm sun on her back melted away her trepidation.

Upon reaching the top of Horgun's Hill, she discovered a shocking sight. Wide stone steps lead down into the hill itself, and at the bottom of the steps a gaping black tunnel yawned up at her. Stunned, Lorelei looked about to see if there was anyone near with whom she could share her discovery, but of course, the lands around the hill stood empty, as they always did. The stones were old and worn and a few scruffy bits of grass grew between some cracks where there was soil for their roots. Small green and red lichens grew on a few of the stones, but they were remarkably clear. Slowly, Lorelei descended the stairs and peered into the dark tunnel. A prickling sensation ran across the base of her neck and her heart pounded.

"Hello," she called into the blackness.

There was no response. The tunnel walls were made of stone and the floor was also lined with stones, and massive blocks of stone formed a roof, which in turn was covered by the dirt and grass of the hill. Lorelei turned and placed a foot on the first step, intending to leave, but some inner force stopped her. A warm wind sprang up and swirled forward out of the tunnel to engulf her, like the great exhalation of some giant beast. Lorelei thought she heard the faint sounds of laughter in that unexplainable wind, and the sound clawed at her heart and reverberated in her mind for several minutes before it faded away. Longing to hear that subtle laughter again and to discover its source, she walked into the tunnel.

She strained to see in the deep gloom, and her heart pounded faster and her thin young muscles tensed. The stones lining the tunnel were cool to the touch and dry, and the tunnel made several sharp turns and grew wider each time until it finally opened into a large cavern that glowed from the light of three large braziers heaped with burning wood. Smoke from the fires rose upwards to slip through large spaces in the rocky ceiling, and Lorelei thought it was odd that she hadn't seen the smoke when she was outside on the hill. She tried to focus, and there was much to see in that ancient cavern; weapons, chests great and small, scrolls and books in small alcoves, and skeletons in larger ones, but Lorelei's gaze was immediately drawn to a glowing figure in front of a throne at the far side of the chamber. It was a woman, standing proud with her hand resting on the pommel of a long-shafted axe with its glittering blade next to her feet. Lorelei immediately dropped to a knee and bowed her head.

"I-I'm sorry, my Lady," she stammered apologetically, and her thin voice echoed into the deep corners and nooks. "I did not mean to intrude on your space. I did not know that anyone lived here. Please forgive me."

Lorelei knelt for several long minutes, and stories about undead wraiths and vampires flooded her mind and made her skin crawl. She remained bowed as her mind brought forth more tales of blood and murder, but she heard no reply from the woman. She pushed the tales of terror out of her thoughts and instead remembered the story about the great hero, Poldrakk, and his fearlessness in the face of danger. With bolstered courage, she looked again at the figure to realize suddenly, that it was only a statue.

She rose and crossed the chamber until she stood before the carven figure, and so lifelike and detailed was the workmanship, that it was hard to believe that the woman was not real. The figure was carved from white marble, and the pale white hue of the skin, which glowed in the firelight, was the only sign that it was not a flesh and blood person. Lorelei gaped in awe as she studied the form. The woman was naked and her breasts were perky and proud, her shoulders were thick and strong, and her slender toes gripped the stone beneath them with uncanny realism. Her hair was cut square above her eyes, but on the sides, it hung down to curl on her shoulders. The strands of hair on her head were carved with extraordinary detail, as were the curling hairs between her thighs. A gentle smirk graced her lips as if she was amused by Lorelei, who looked with shock upon her bravado and nakedness. Veins stood out on her strong arms, and her hand rested on the axe handle with the casual confidence of a warrior. The statue's eyes were inlaid with polished gems that gave them an ethereal realness, and a shiver ran through Lorelei and she suddenly thought this woman might be a golem, and she might spring to life at any moment. And hung around the statue's neck was a gruesome sight; a string of human skulls. These had yellowed with age and were clearly real and not carved from stone. They grinned at Lorelei with their grim countenances, but she held fast and did not flinch, and instead, she reached out her young hand and touched a marble thigh.

She smiled as she caressed the smooth marble, but a sudden deep grunt caused her to spin and stumble with fright. She bent her legs and prepared to flee, and for the first time, she noticed that she was not alone in the cavernous hall. Not ten yards away was a stone bench, and on that bench was a man. He sat tall with his hands resting on his thighs and he studied Lorelei with burning blue eyes. His pants were dark crimson and he wore fur-skin boots. He was shirtless, and his skin was dark and taunt from a life spent in the burning sun. His grey hair hung down his back in a long braid, his grey beard was trimmed short, and the wrinkles on his face told Lorelei that he was old, yet his muscled torso was still strong and full, like a man in the prime of life. Gold rings hung from his ears and several necklaces of glittering gems set in gold clasps sat on his broad chest. Lorelei's eyes moved from the treasure he wore to the numerous scars which adorned his whole body, including scars on both cheeks and his forehead.

Instead of being terrified by this savage man, Lorelei felt oddly comforted that she was not alone in the chamber, and she stood tall before him, not wanting to show fear.

The man tilted his head and studied her for a long while before speaking. "You must be gentle in your reverence for her," he said with a gravelly voice as he motioned to the statue.

Lorelei looked up at the woman with her brazen grin and exposed body. "Who is she?"

43

"You look upon Kurga, mortal Queen of Lord Reh, the ancient God of Battle, forgotten by most though his power has not lessened with the churning ages."

"Your words are a mystery to me," said Lorelei. "I know nothing of these beings."

"Kurga walked this earth three millennia ago," said the man. "She was a Goddess of blood and steel, and her devotion to Lord Reh was so great that she became his consort and now she resides in the immortal realm that is separate from our own. I could tell you about the adventures and glory of Kurga, but I don't think I should. You show courage, young one, but the knowledge I possess could wither your soul and destroy your body."

"Tell me!" barked Lorelei with a ferocity that she didn't know she possessed. She clenched her small fists and trembled at her own boldness and the reaction it might illicit.

"I must know who she was!" she said after several moments of unbearable silence.

"You must, or you want?" smirked the man. "Curiosity and need are separate things, though they both drive men mad with desperation."

Lorelei remained silent and looked again upon the stature before returning her gaze to the man.

"I am commanded by none, save Kurga," he whispered with a smile. "And I wonder, who is your God, child?"

Lorelei's brow furrowed and she shook her head. "The people of this island have several, but I have none," she said. "I find no enlightenment in the harvest or the wind and the rain. I do not hate those things, but I also find no spirits in them. It cannot be an accident that I stumbled into this forbidden chamber. I want to know why you are here. What is this forgotten idol? Why do you watch over it? Who was she? How could she have the power to command men, even now? I cannot leave without knowing. I beg you, tell me about your Gods. Tell me about Kurga. I need to know."

The man slowly stood up and he towered over Lorelei, and the braziers seemed to grow and crackle, and flashes of light danced across the stone walls and across his scarred body. Lorelei's heart pounded and her lips quivered with an excitement she had never known.

"This is not an easy thing you ask of me," he said. "Knowledge comes at a cost, and the price to know Kurga is steep. It is the ultimate price, do you understand? You are young and foolhardy, and I would tell you to flee and forget this place. I would say go home to your soft bed and peaceful life, but you speak with conviction. There is a fire in you that I recognize. I know it all too well. It consumes me as it does you. Do you truly understand the cost of what you ask? Think carefully before answering. Are you willing to give up everything in search of answers?"

Lorelei licked her dry lips and looked into his deep blue eyes, and she spoke with a voice that was firm but nearly silent. "Aye," she whispered.

The man took a step toward her and her heart pounded faster. She studied his many scars and his thick muscles, and then she looked up into his glowing eyes which held her fast for what seemed like an eternity. Finally, he nodded and smiled to himself.

"Very well," he said. "I am Zuda, last berserker of the great cult of Kurga. I will train you, child, and teach you about my Gods. But hear my words! You now tread the path of blood! The path of Kurga, Goddess of Death and Queen of Lord Reh the everlasting! She, who is first and deadliest of all berserkers, offers you wisdom beyond the ken of other mortals! If you abandon her, I will kill you. If you fail in your training, you will die." Zuda bowed his head towards the great statue. "I swear this to you, my Queen. This girl will learn your ways or die in the process."

Lorelei's mind screamed at her to run before it was too late, but her soul rejected reason in favor of the mad words of the barbarian, Zuda, and she turned to face the glowing marble.

45

"Guide me, great Kurga," said Lorelei, and she bowed her head. "I will not fail you; I swear it."

"Good," said Zuda, and he crossed the chamber a grabbed a thick iron bar. "You will return every morning without question. If you are not here at sunrise, I will find you, and I will kill you."

"Agreed," said Lorelei.

Zuda tossed the bar at Lorelei's feet. It cracked the flagstones when it landed and Lorelei cringed at the ringing sound it made. "Lift the iron," said Zuda.

Lorelei bent down and tried to grab the thick bar, but her soft hands could not grasp it and she strained and pulled, but she could barely budge it. "I-I can't lift it," she gasped.

"Not yet," grunted Zuda. "But you will. You are soft from the fields, and you must become hard like that iron if you are to survive the world that Kurga will show you. We will train."

Lorelei watched Zuda walk to a large alcove and grab more iron objects. She steadied herself and did as she was told, and the firelight glowed against her pale skin, glistening with sweat, and she raised small iron bars above her head and mirrored Zuda's movements. And as she struggled, the world around her grew vague and incorporeal, and a sudden shock of pain pulled Lorelei back into the present.

Lorelei tugged at the biting rope around her neck and clawed at the clover around her feet, and she wheezed and drooled and her eyes burned. The pale werewolf gave a great tug and Lorelei was jerked off her knees. The wolf bounded forward and it struck her with its inhuman strength and she nearly passed out again. She coughed up blood and her arms shook, and she feared that at any moment fanged jaws would close upon her and she would be helpless to fight back as she was changed into a beast. She could already feel her body distorting and rupturing in grotesque ways as it was destroyed, remade, and enslaved. But no fangs pierced her flesh, and suddenly, Lorelei's mind crystalized on her memory of the great marble statue of Kurga. She saw the smirking face and curling hair, and the glittering eyes. Lorelei focused on that image in her mind and slowly some clarity began to return, and she realized that her hand was resting on something firm amidst the clover and nettles. It was the handle of her sword and gripping it steadied her arms. She looked up at the filthy back of the pale werewolf, but the beast ignored her and watched its fellows battle Torgerd.

Lorelei stared with agony through enflamed and bloodshot eyes, as Torgerd was gashed across her back by a darting wolf, and then again across the thigh by a second wolf. She was growing too weak and slow to fight off the circling dogs, and they paced in a great circle, like horrific vultures tightening around soon-to-be dead meat.

With blood and spit oozing from her gritted teeth, Lorelei swung her sword and cut through one of the white werewolf's legs. It toppled over backward with a surprised grunt and Lorelei quickly silenced it with a savage blow that cut deep into the wolf's throat. It's disgusting clawed hands twitched and groped at the sky, and its blood gurgled out of the wound and coated its pale fur and soaked into the heather beneath it, and in a matter of seconds, it was dead. Lorelei loosened the rope as her hands grew steadier, and she freed herself from the noose and was surprised to see that her murder had gone unnoticed as the battle with Torgerd drew the full attention of the pack. The black werewolf was nearest to her and it watched like a commander and howled as its pack took turns assailing the struggling but resolute Torgerd.

Lorelei wiped the frothing drool from her mouth and lifted her broadsword. With the steel firmly in her grasp, she began to regain her focus, and she stood up on wobbly legs. She paused for only a second to center her balance, and then she lunged forward into the battle and rammed her sword through the back of the great black wolf. The blade

47

exploded out of the front of the wolf's torso, crimson and covered in gore and bits of fur. The werewolf coughed up thick clumps of blood, then it spun around and its long hairy arm bashed Lorelei in the head and sent her reeling. Her legs were still too weak from the poison, and though she tried to remain upright, the force from the blow was too much and she tumbled into the dark clover. The werewolf howled at the stars and ignored the sword through its body, and then its husky voice barked at Lorelei.

"Stay down, wench," it said. "Your time will come soon. You will become one of us, and you will bear my pups to swell our legions. Be grateful that I have a use for you, human scum."

The black werewolf turned back towards Torgerd, who still fought valiantly to keep the remaining pack at bay. "Kill this barbarian," he barked. "We must feast on her flesh and then return to the dens!"

Lorelei would not stand for the wolf's latest insult and she raged on the ground and seethed, and she cloaked herself in a wave of white-hot anger that burned away the last effects of the poison in her veins. She pulled off her blue shirt and exposed her bare skin to the night air, and the feeling sent needles of adrenaline coursing through her thick muscles, and her arms flexed with a desire to slay.

The hellish eyes of the black wolf turned to face Lorelei, and its long arms pulled the sword free from its body. Blood squirted from the wound for only a moment, but it quickly stopped as the wolf's body began to heal. The wolf laughed and dropped the sword into the clover and Lorelei stood tall and faced it.

"You fucking mutt," she snarled.

The werewolf stopped laughing and pounced forward jaws agape. Lorelei's booted feet bounded through the clover towards the wolf, and at the last minute, she dropped to her side and slid under the lunging beast and between its legs. The wolf tumbled forward and snapped its jaws with anger, and it spun around to find Lorelei, sword in hand, charging again. Demonic black claws shot forward towards Lorelei's face, but the fiendish arm was severed mid-forearm before it reached her. The werewolf had never encountered such speed before, and he howled with surprise as the sword's return stroke bit heavily across his midsection. His remaining claws swung downward and cut across Lorelei's shoulder, but she was already lunging past his attack. With a grunt, she stabbed upward through his exposed armpit, and her steel passed through muscles and lungs. The wolf reacted with violent quickness and its heavy elbow slammed into Lorelei's head and knocked her over.

Ignoring the pain in her head, Lorelei grinned with murderous satisfaction as the werewolf writhed and struggled, unable to pull the sword from its body with its one remaining hand. It quickly gave up trying to remove the steel barb, and instead, it leapt forward and cloaked the prone berserker with its great form. The wolf's eyes bulged, as did the veins on its neck, as it pushed its face towards Lorelei's bare flesh with all its might. She fought back and her iron limbs pressed against the wolf's throat, trying to keep it at bay. But her strength and effort were slowly being overtaken by the supernatural power of the beast, and with each passing moment, the fangs of death inched closer.

The werewolf's jaws were so close that its long, saliva-coated tongue slipped forward and began to hungrily run itself over Lorelei's exposed breasts. She growled with revulsion and the wolf grinned with pleasure, its ultimate victory near at hand.

With a final burst of energy, Lorelei released one of her hands and she ran it down the wolf's torso until she found the first wound that she had given the beast. Upon finding that still unhealed gash, she plunged her hand deep into the wolf's body, and her arm muscles tensed with power as she found what she sought. The wolf redoubled its efforts and its severed arm pressed against her face, but Lorelei pulled hard, and with a scream, she broke a long rib and ripped it free. And as fresh wolf blood gushed onto her, she stabbed the rib upwards into the wolf's neck. The beast tried to pull away, but Lorelei wrapped her legs around its waist and held it tight, and with both hands, she used the rib to tear a great gash through the wolf's throat. Then she released her legs and kicked the werewolf away to thrash about on the ground as its life spilled out of its half-severed head.

Lorelei moved forward quickly, and with power coursing through her thighs she straddled the wolf's back, and her hands locked onto its chin and one of its shaggy ears. A great yell escaped her snarling mouth and her hard body flexed and pulled, and the wolf's head was jerked around with such force that its neck broke in several places, and its muscles and sinews split and ruptured. A low gurgle leaked from its dying maw and Lorelei's pent-up rage became a roar, and she triumphantly spit in the face of the helpless wolf.

The rest of the pack was startled by Lorelei's exclamation, and they gaped as she ripped her sword free and hacked at the black wolf until his head came free. The headless body clawed feebly at the ground, searching for its head, but Lorelei tossed the grim object far away, and then she planted a foot firmly on the back of the corpse as it finally died, and she smiled at the remaining wolves who now seemed unsure. The killing had aroused her and her nipples stood firm, and her body was covered in the blood of the beast, and she stabbed at the hairy body beneath her and waved her gore-covered blade at the other werewolves.

"Your pack is undone, foul dogs," she hissed. "I'll water this turf with your blood, and then I'll howl in triumph and claim your hunting grounds as my own. Flea-ridden vermin! Come at me, if you dare!"

Two werewolves broke from the circle around Torgerd and charged Lorelei. The first wolf misjudged its attack as Lorelei counter-charged, and her sword cut through its ear and then into its thick sinuous neck. It stumbled with a whine as its blood gushed from the wound to quickly mat its tan fur. Lorelei followed through with a crushing blow that spilled brains into the clover. The second wolf leapt over its dead companion and its claws raked against Lorelei's steel, and she was nearly spun about by the power behind its savage blows.

The reprieve in the number of foes assailing Torgerd had given her new strength, and her mighty axe fell in devastating arcs that severed wolf limbs and mangled wolf bodies, and the ferocity of her vengeance left two butchered mounds of flesh and fur in the heather, steaming in the cool night air. Torgerd grunted with satisfaction as she looked at her handiwork, but her blood loss finally overcame her and she fell to her knees with a groan.

Meanwhile, Lorelei's sword cut deeply through the thighs of the last wolf, felling it, and as it looked up at her from its back, she stabbed it through the stomach. She pulled her sword free and prepared to kill the dog, but it began to shift and twitch unexpectantly. It coughed up foul blood and mucus, and its body shrunk, and it urinated profusely, and it shed its fur until the wolf was gone and a dwarf with a blonde beard looked up at her. His wounds were already partially healed from the transformation, and he sweated and panted. He flashed his best smile and waved a dirty hand.

"Mercy, great Lady," he said. "I beg of you, spare me. I respect your ferocity. You have my leave to travel in these hills. Go where thou wilt. The wolves of Blyddugh will not harry you. My word is bond, yes? Let us part without further blood. I will call off my clan."

For a moment Lorelei seemed to consider the dwarf's plea, and his shoulders relaxed and he continued to smile. Lorelei lowered her sword and flicked it at the dwarf so that blood was flung from the blade onto his naked torso. The bright moonlight reflected off her sweating breasts and a single stream of crimson fluid dripped from her collarbone to give the appearance that her central skull tattoo was crying blood. The dwarf watched the blood roll down her chest and his smile faded as her hard muscles flexed with rage and power.

"I have your leave, do I?" sneered Lorelei. "I don't need it, dog. I go where I will in this world, and I do what I want! No one commands me, and no one enslaves me!"

Lorelei's sword flashed and the dwarf raised his hands in defense, but it was to no avail. Steel, guided by her powerful muscles, sheared through his arms, and hacked into his chest. His severed limbs were flung about grotesquely as he turned over and tried to crawl away through the clover, leaving a shining red trail in the matted turf. Lorelei stalked behind him and let him crawl for a few paces before she struck again, and again, and again until the dwarf's body lay in multiple pieces and her slaughter-lust was sated.

With a sudden jerk, Lorelei pulled herself away from her butchery and looked about frantically for her companion. Torgerd was some yards away, on her knees with her head bowed. Lorelei ran to her, and as she neared, Torgerd collapsed onto her broad back. Lorelei tossed her sword and began to study Torgerd's wounds.

"Hold fast, sister," she said with genuine concern. And then she ran to find their traveling packs. Torgerd smiled weakly at Lorelei when she returned with their supplies.

"Those dogs thought we were lost lambs, easy for the plucking," grinned Torgerd. "Ha! Their flesh cut as smooth as any other. Foul demons, but Odindisa be praised, we showed them the sharpness of our steel and the strength of our arms."

Lorelei smiled with Torgerd and worked quickly to stop her bleeding and wrap her various wounds. "Aye," she said softly. "No dogs will howl over these hills tonight."

After her wounds were wrapped and she drank a prodigious amount of water, Torgerd felt good enough to stand again. At Lorelei's command, she held back while Lorelei piled the werewolves and set fire to their corpses. The greasy fur burned easily and the companions walked to another hill to avoid the stench before they built their own small fire and made camp. Lorelei kept the head of the black werewolf and put it into a sack, a grim trophy of their ordeal.

After scouting about, Lorelei found a stream of clean water and she removed her pants and washed the blood from her skin and clothes, sending a thick crimson cloud trickling away through the hills. She returned to the hilltop and laid her clothes near the fire to dry, and then she unwrapped some of Torgerd's bandages and began to stitch shut the deepest cuts. Torgerd remained silent as her flesh was pierced and pulled back together. She had been stitched many times before and she knew it was the best way to stop from bleeding to death. Afterward, clean bandages were applied and fresh wood was thrown on the fire.

"I will take first watch," said Lorelei as she lounged in the firelight and stretched her naked legs before her. She ran a hand down her stomach and rested it on her mound. "I am aroused and full of energy."

Torgerd nodded with a grunt of approval and laid down near the fire to sleep.

"Thank you," said Lorelei. "You kept the beasts at bay while I was left mad and without control of my body. You saved me."

"Hmph," shrugged Torgerd. "You would have saved yourself, little savage, I am sure. Those bastards would have pranced and preened all night, and only when your sword was in their stomach would they have realized their mistake."

"Perhaps," said Lorelei quietly and without conviction. She studied Torgerd for a few minutes as the big barbarian yawned and closed her eyes.

"You remind me of my oldest sister, Gwendolyn," whispered Lorelei.

Torgerd smirked, "Did she also protect you from calamity most foul?"

"Yes," smiled Lorelei. "But only from the exasperations of our parents, or from my own foolishness."

"Well, we could use her wisdom in these dark hills," chuckled Torgerd. "Let's hope you learned from her guidance, berserker. I doubt these dogs will be the only test we face ere we reach our horrid destination."

"Aye," said Lorelei, and she looked at the stars above and smiled as she thought about her sisters on the Blue Isle. She thought about the frolicking goats and the meadows and picking berries and harvesting honey. She thought about Horgun's Hill and how beautiful it was when the wildflowers were in bloom across its ancient surface. Then she bit her lip and thought about young Castor and the rousing time they spent together. She moaned gently and absently watched the flames as her hand gyrated inside her moist flesh and caused her strong legs to lift and spread and flex.

5. Sellswords

Dappled sunlight pulsed down through strange clouds as Lorelei and Torgerd continued westward through the Black Hills. The demon's blood, won through sorcery and slaughter, still moved through their veins, and though it was nearly spent, it helped speed Torgerd's recovery. The small mounded hills slowly gave way to longer rolling hillsides and sporadic groves of trees. The very air around them grew strange, and the hair on Lorelei's neck bristled at each new scent and sound. No beasts or birds crossed their path and they walked in silence, alert, and with hands gripping sword hilts.

After several hours of silent travel, Lorelei turned a somber gaze onto her companion. "Torgerd," she began quietly, "when we met in the Pit you uttered the names of Reh and Kurga. You are the first I have met in my long travels to know those names. How is that so?"

Torgerd sighed heavily and gathered her thoughts, and a palpable tension grew between them, though it was not built of anger, but rather of the trepidation caused by preparing to share a great burden.

"During the long winter nights my people huddle in great halls and huts," said Torgerd. "And the elders tell rousing tales of heroes and gods, wizards and monsters. On one such evening, our King told us about the oldest of the ancient Demons and Gods that once walked the world, including Ugada the Mad and Reh the Bloodthirsty. The story of Reh was meant as a warning, for he said that Reh's berserkers could still be found wandering the world, and they were foes not to be underestimated. That warning rang true years later when I faced such a man while at war in the east. Wild he was, like a mad dog, and his nakedness was bold and unexpected. He killed many warriors before I split his skull."

Torgerd paused and a painful memory seemed to cross her face before she continued. "As for Kurga," she said slowly. "It was a night of extreme cold and I was alone in the hut of our great wise-woman, Muab. A queen she could have been had she wished it, but she preferred to be a keeper of knowledge and she was renowned far and wide for her wisdom. On this bitter evening, she burned the incense heavy and stoked the fire hard, and she said she needed to tell me a tale that she had never told anyone else in her long life. She said it was forbidden knowledge, about the days when the elder gods mingled with mortals, and how the world was scarred by the lust of such couplings. And so, she sang to me a song..."

"The lay of Kurga," interrupted Lorelei with a whisper.

"Aye," said Torgerd somberly. "So, you do know it?"

"Yes," said Lorelei. "I know all of it and more. Much more."

"Well, the little I heard was too much for me," said Torgerd. "The wise woman wept openly as she sang with her brittle voice, and the pain of her torment cut me like a dagger. She, who had fought generations of raiders, and had slain the cursed bears of Gormund, and destroyed the sea witch of Iffenbydd! Even she could not withstand the legend of Kurga, most terrible of all the berserkers of Reh. After the song, she never spoke again in life. She lays now in honor, in a great barrow fit for only the finest heroes and kings of men."

Torgerd stopped walking and looked hard at Lorelei. "When I saw you in the Pit, I remembered the song of Kurga, and my heart ached for vengeance, but it also tightened with fear. Fear such as I have never felt in battle."

Torgerd reached out and gently brushed away the blonde hair that blew across Lorelei's emerald eyes. "I no longer seek vengeance," she said. "But I still fear you, Lorelei, disciple of Kurga, Queen of berserkers. I fear you. But I also trust you."

"Although, I don't know if I should trust myself," continued Torgerd, and she tapped her chest with her fist. "I died in the Pit, yet I still live. Is this a new life I wield or a continuation of the previous one? The world is new to my eyes but also the same. It makes no sense. Am I still the same woman I was? Do I need to be?"

Lorelei had no answers for her companion. She simply gripped Torgerd's shoulder to show solidarity with her struggle.

They walked on in silence for a while until Torgerd spoke again. "The superstitions of my people sit heavily on my shoulders, and I struggle to overthrow them. Pay no mind to my rambling. I was born a fisherwoman, after all."

Lorelei smiled and shrugged her thick shoulders. "I was born a goat herder," she said.

The look of surprise on Torgerd's face sent Lorelei into a fit of laughter, and after a minute, Torgerd joined her, and their mirth drove away the last lingering shadows from the previous night.

They traveled in silence the rest of the day and into the next, and as the afternoon wore away, they began to hear voices on the wind, and gruff laughter, and the sounds of iron working and the neighing of ponies. The land had changed again, and it was full of shrubs and wild thickets, and a few ancient gnarly trees that lifted near-dead branches high into the air. With the brush as cover, the women cautiously approached the source of the sounds, and after cresting a broad hill, they found themselves looking down into the ruins of a once great structure. A castle it might have been, or a walled town, it was hard to discern because it had been reduced to small sporadic bits of stonework, which would in turn give way to larger sections of remaining walls. The whole site was still enclosed with a tall but crumbling outer wall. Vines and moss grew heavy on the stonework, and much of the ancient mortar had eroded, and it was clear that none of the walls reached their original height.

Many of the hollow ruins had makeshift wooden roofs thrown over their crumbling walls, and some even had cloth drapes covering windows or rough wooden shutters. Doors had also been fashioned from planks and thrown across these squalid dwellings. There was a great hustle and bustle of activity outside the huts, and many dwarves walked to and fro with heavy baskets on their broad backs or wheelbarrows careening around in front of their quick steps. There were many small groups of dwarves huddled around little fires, heating tea or stew, as they whispered in gruff tones about the business that brought them to this chaotic center of mercantilism. Larger beings also walked among the dwarves, and they were grim figures, human-like but taller, with large sloping brows and pronounced jaws with protruding canines. The legs of these ogres were too short and their arms too long, and many had brutal clubs and cleavers hanging from leather belts.

The road into the camp passed through what must have once been the entrance to the walled town. Crumbling sections of the gateway still stood, with guard houses on either side of a wide portal. A small remnant of an arch still rose above the entrance, telling of a much grander structure that had existed centuries ago. Thorn bushes and tall shrubs grew thickly along the walls. And inside the northern guard house, a small fire belched smoke, and two figures could be seen moving about.

The encampment seemed harmless enough, but for two humans seeking treasure, it could quickly become a death trap. They could easily conceal themselves in the underbrush and pass it by, but Lorelei had other plans, riskier, but useful as well. She knew that no single fighter in the camp could stand against her or Torgerd, but the dwarves could probably overwhelm them with sheer strength of numbers, and with poisons and darts, which the dwarves were known for. A hundred small wounds could bring down the mightiest warrior, and the whole camp would be aroused quickly should they attack any dwarf in the open. The ogres would also be a problem, as they were fearless and savage and strong.

Lorelei rubbed a hand across her smooth sharp chin as she debated with herself over the best course of action. Finally, she took off her pack and left it with Torgerd, and she made her way down the hill, clinging to the shadows. She crept along the wall and moved around the shrubs and brambles, crawling, when necessary, until she was near the guard house. She crouched in front of the rotting centipede-infested wall and pulled her cloak tight over her body. She flicked a small rock and it hit the side of the stone guard house. She waited a moment and then flicked another rock. When the third rock hit the hut, one of the guards stepped out to look about. It was one of the ogres, and his small dark eyes looked out over yellowed canines that stuck out of his protruding ape-like jaw. It took a few minutes, but the guard eventually saw the hunched and cloaked form of Lorelei. The guard scratched his hairy chin and walked forward to investigate. He could not tell if the cloak covered an abandoned traveling pack or a sleeping dwarf. His gnarly hand reached down and pulled the cloak, and that's when Lorelei pounced, and she leapt upwards and her long dagger ripped through the ogre's neck. It stumbled and grabbed at its bleeding throat and Lorelei cut again, even deeper into the veins and sinews under its jaw. She deftly avoided the spray of blood and grabbed the slumping body, and carefully pulled its mass deep into the bushes. She grabbed a heavy cleaver from the dead ogre's belt and moved towards the guard house, deadly and silent like a panther on the prowl.

Lorelei peered into the stone chamber and watched a dwarf with a long beard as he stirred a pot that was suspended over a fire. Then he snorted and stepped to the corner of the chamber, and he pulled out his penis and urinated against the stones. When he finished, he kicked some dirty straw towards the corner and went back to watching the pot. Lorelei pulled her hood down and pushed back her cloak behind her shoulders, and she unbuttoned her shirt and exposed her breasts seductively. And then she stepped into the doorway with her chest protruding forward and the cleaver concealed behind her back.

"What?" mumbled the dwarf in surprise, but not alarm. "A woman, is it? A human woman? Not seen one of your ilk around here in many a year." His shining eyes focused on Lorelei's exposed skin and he instinctively rubbed his crotch. "Garsh, would you look at that. Perfect as you please, a real treat."

Lorelei stepped closer and the dwarf snorted again and smiled with black rotting teeth. "Has Gunby sent you here?" asked the dwarf. "A reward for poor old Fimm, who always gets the longest watch in this lonely chamber."

"Yes," whispered Lorelei.

"Haha," chuckled Fimm, and he rubbed his hands heartily. "Well, let's see what you're about. Take off that cloak, wench."

Fimm's smile never had a chance to diminish, as Lorelei's speed and power hacked the cleaver through his grinning face until it was stopped by his thick collarbone. The dwarf's body spasmed and slumped, and blood leaked in a steady stream from the red line that had been cut from his scalp to his chest, where the cleaver's handle now stuck out like a hellish doorknob, collecting crimson muck that fell from the ruined visage above it.

Lorelei buttoned her shirt and she poked her head out of the chamber and whistled like a sparrow, and a few minutes later, Torgerd came forward from the bushes.

"Now what?" asked the red-haired barbarian.

"We go into the camp," said Lorelei. "They will study us but assume that the guards let us through. Best to remain cloaked, though. If we must, we will carve a bloody trail out of this filthy hole, but wandering aimlessly in this fey land does not appeal to me. We need to find someone who will give us information, without asking too many questions. And we must be quick, too. When they find this fellow, hopefully they will assume his missing companion did the deed. But it's best not to trust in that for too long."

"I follow your lead, Berserker," said Torgerd.

With cloaks and hoods drawn tight, the women sauntered into the camp. They passed many tents and huddled dwarves deep in talk or sweating over fires, and their hidden hands gripped their daggers. Lorelei's emerald eyes scanned the bustling throng, looking for an opportunity. Dwarves glanced up at them as they passed, and a few let their inquisitive gazes linger, but most forgot them quickly. At the center of the camp, the space widened and the ruins were less dense. This had clearly been a grand courtyard in its past glory, though now it was a wretched place full of detritus and filth, and crude smells. A mass of dwarves in the center of the courtyard crowded around and formed a makeshift ring, inside of which, two naked ogres pummeled one another with swollen bloody fists. Their faces were covered with ugly bruises and blood, and though they staggered from fatigue, their knuckles continued to pulp each other's flesh.

Torgerd turned to Lorelei. "Care to try your luck," she smirked.

"Another time," smiled Lorelei.

Just then a pair of dwarves armed with halberds approached them. The lead dwarf, with a long-braided beard and a red bandana across his balding head, held out a hand.

"Ho, there," he grunted. "Who are you and what is your purpose in Sulfrod?"

"We are travelers, in search of work," said Lorelei. "The same as many others."

"Others are half as tall, and welcome here," said the dwarf. "You are neither."

The second dwarf tightened his grip on his halberd, and Lorelei fingered her concealed dagger. A few more dwarves approached the women with their thick hands resting on short swords at their hips.

"We come to trade and sell," said Lorelei. "Goods, but mostly services. We were told we would find work here."

"And what work do you do, she-mongrel? Business spent on your back and knees I'll wager."

61

The gathering dwarves chuckled. Lorelei growled, and slowly she unslung a large bag, and she reached inside, and the dwarves gasped in astonishment as she withdrew the head of the black werewolf. Its tongue dangled from its rotting mouth, and Lorelei held the grisly thing above the heads of the dwarves. Their mirth was driven from them under the dead eyes of the wolf, and they began to disperse until only the first two remained.

"This is my business," Lorelei hissed. "Do you wish to test me?"

The dwarf wiped a hand on his bandana and then he lifted his halberd. "Mind how you go," he said dangerously before he turned and walked away, his companion in tow.

Lorelei replaced the head in the sack, and Torgerd huddled close.

"How do we pry answers from the lips of these suspicious bastards?"

As if in reply to Torgerd's question, a whistle cut the tense air. The women looked over towards a mass of huts with new timber strung across rotting stone walls. A black-bearded dwarf stood next to a closed doorway and he waved the women over. They approached cautiously, with eyes searching the shadows of the alleys and closed windows, alert for bolts and poisoned darts that could be flung at them from hidden murder holes.

"A fine trophy you flash about," said the dwarf. "Dangerous to do so, but impressive."

"What do you want?" asked Lorelei.

"That depends entirely on what *you* want," said the dwarf cryptically. "Most of this lot are miners or laborers or gem smiths. Some are prostitutes and some are thieves, and many are slaves to some vice or another. I wonder which you are, to come so boldly into Sulfrod. Are you seeking to join the downtrodden masses before you, or are you seeking loftier employ?"

"Our talents would be wasted in a mine," smiled Lorelei. "And our confidence comes from the steel we carry, and what we like to do with it."

62

"Ah," grinned the dwarf knowingly. "Sellswords, eh? I thought as much. Well, you're talking to the right dwarf, yes you are." He glanced about with squinted eyes and then he spit a large wad of tobacco on the ground. He motioned with his head towards the hut behind him. He opened the door and went inside, and the women followed.

Torgerd quietly bolted the door once they were inside the hut. Several dwarves sat around a table sorting coins and gems, and they only briefly glanced at the tall strangers. A fire crackled in a pit in the center of the room, and boxes and sacks were piled against the walls along with an assortment of swords and daggers and crossbows. The black-haired dwarf waved the women over to an unoccupied corner where they dropped their packs and peeled off their cloaks. The corner was stacked with long boxes, like coffins, with curious writing on the sides. One box near Lorelei had no lid, and a mummified body could be seen. A thin gold band was pressed around the head, outside of the tight pale wrappings that covered the mummy. These dwarves were graverobbers. Lorelei bristled at the thought.

The dwarf reached into the crate and roughly pulled the band off the wrapped head, snapping the aged neck in the process. He tossed the band across the room and another dwarf caught it and added it to the pile on the table.

"To business," said the dwarf, refocusing on the women. "My name is Hugo. You can call me Boss if ya wish. I need some fresh muscle if you got the skill. That wolf head tells me you do. I could hire a band of ogres, but they're too stupid for the delicate work we do. Got a big job coming up. On our way to the Vale of Plursotch, and then we sail around the coast and go inland to Jutt. Those damned wizards pay well for these bodies. Guard the stock and watch our backs, and I'll make you rich."

Lorelei and Torgerd shared a glance and the dwarf studied them closely.

"What do you say," he mused. "I can pay 2 drags a day, plus 5 percent of the bounty, plus food and drink. It's the best offer you'll get in this damned camp, I guarantee it."

"Any obstacles?" smirked Lorelei.

Hugo grinned and chuckled. "Might be," he said. "Some scattered villages and farmers mostly. They don't take lightly to our business, and if they spot us, you'll need to take care of them. And sometimes we might need some nosy passersby silenced. Nothing that you can't handle, I'm sure. And if'n you need a bit of murder and pillage too, then that's okay, so long as it doesn't disrupt our primary business."

"Why Plursotch?" asked Lorelei, and she stretched her shoulders casually. "Why not plunder the serpent temples and the great pyramid? It must have hundreds of tombs, all of them full of bodies, and I hear it's practically unguarded. West of here, isn't it? We could search it before going to Plursotch. With our help, I'm sure you could find a much richer vein of corpses to exploit in those ancient tombs."

Hugo stiffened at the mention of serpents and looked about nervously. "You're well informed, for a human," he began, "but still stupid. Firstly, those tombs are northwest of here, not west. Secondly, no one approaches that territory if they value their skin." Hugo spit on the floor and the vile goo splashed across Lorelei's boot. "I don't know if the tales are true, and my bones tell me that they're probably a bunch of lies. But I ain't gunna be the first to go prove it. Maybe there is no snake goddess, and maybe that temple isn't lost in some enchanted grove, and maybe the time has come to plunder that ancient land, but I ain't dumb enough to go and see what's what. I do know that land is full of elves and mad beasts, that is certain. And those elves are degenerate scum, and there ain't no money in dying and possibly being eaten by their Queen, curse her filthy scales if she's even real."

"But in Plursotch," smiled Hugo, "we have secret mines and maps to forgotten graveyards, and dumb peasants that we can trick or kill, and the guarantee of a hefty return."

The dwarf and the women shared hard glances for several minutes. Finally, Hugo spit again and smiled.

"Well, what'll it be?" he said. "Are you in?"

"Aye," said Lorelei. "Your terms are acceptable."

"Good, good," said Hugo, and he rubbed his hands and slapped his thighs. "The rest of the crew will be back soon and we leave in two days."

Torgerd began to walk across the room towards the other dwarves around the table, moving slowly, with casual steps. Lorelei relaxed and stretched her neck, and she waved her firm butt towards the dwarf seductively and gave him a wink. Hugo licked his cracked lips and stepped up close to her, and his meaty hand ran up the back of her leg and then firmly groped her backside.

"If you want extra pay," said Hugo hungrily, "I can arrange that. It gets mighty lonely on the road." His hand groped deeper between her cheeks. "An extra 2 drags a night, eh? For you and your friend."

Lorelei turned to face Hugo, and she began to unbutton her shirt, and with excitement, Hugo's dirty hands pawed at her crotch and thighs. Lorelei parted her shirt, and Hugo's hungry eyes froze on the skull tattoo that faced him. Then he looked up into her eyes, and he was met by emerald orbs filled with hate and power. He took a step backward and raised his hands.

"Hold on," he pleaded. "My mistake."

But Lorelei was already moving, and she grabbed his head and slammed it into her knee, and with a crash, Hugo fell backward into the crates of mummies, knocking some to the floor. The other dwarves were startled by the sound and pulled away from their work, and Torgerd drew her sword and laid into them, and she hewed off two heads while their

65

bodies remained seated. Blood pulsed across the table to mix with the gems and gold, and the other two dwarves grabbed weapons and prepared to fight. Torgerd was more than ready for them, and she crushed the closest dwarf with a chair and then stabbed his unconscious body. And then she chased down the last dwarf and hacked through his spine as he ran for the door. He moaned and twitched on the floor until Torgerd's blade pierced his heart.

In the corner, Lorelei reached into the nearest crate and gripping the jaw of a half-unwrapped mummy, she ripped the petrified skull free from its linen and leather bonds. She hovered over Hugo, a shadow of death that he had unwittingly unleashed upon himself.

The dwarf shook his terrified head. "10 percent of the bounty," he whimpered. "More than fair. What say you?"

Lorelei's blood was hot and she sneered at the cowering dwarf. "It's not enough," she hissed. Then she swung the skull against Hugo's own hard head, and her murderous blows struck him over and over, until his skull cracked from the torment, and his head was reduced to mush. Afterward, she placed the petrified skull back into the crate with its mishandled body. She cracked open a shuttered window in the corner of the hut and looked outside into an empty alley space. Then, she bent over the dwarves' fire and grabbed several enflamed logs, and began tossing them around the hut. She dropped two against the mummy crates, and they were quickly engulfed in flames.

"Your souls are free to go where you will," said Lorelei. "Curses upon those that defiled you."

Torgerd climbed out the window and then Lorelei handed her their gear, and then she climbed out, just as the timbers of the roof caught fire. Outside, shouts were beginning and the camp was stirring at the news of a fire. The companions quickly moved north, staying in the alleys, and working their way through the vast ruins and crumbling stones. Dwarfs and ogres ran about and the yelling was furious and urgent. The flames from the burning hut threatened to spread to nearby structures, and in short order, the whole camp and its varied cargoes could be turned to ash.

The commotion and confusion allowed the women to reach the edge of the camp without further confrontation, and as they slipped past the last overgrown piece of rotting outer wall, a strange sight greeted them. They saw a broad fenced enclosure, and inside was a curious beast. Its shoulders stood as tall as a large horse, but its body was thick and rough, and its legs were like mighty pillars, and its head was massive and long, and upon that mighty snout rose two great horns, and the front horn was twice as long as the one behind it. The skin of the beast was black as coal, and iron rings were clasped around its front legs and these were chained to large stakes driven into the ground. Ogres circled the beast with wooden staffs, and they beat it and yelled, and the beast stomped and snorted and threatened to trample the ogres, if only it could get free of the chains.

"What is that monster?" queried Torgerd in awe.

"A rhino," said Lorelei. "They live far to the south, beyond Krillso, the Great Red Sea. I have seen herds of them west of Pyra and all down the Crimson Coast. But never have I seen one so large, and so black of color."

"Another trophy stolen by these damned dwarfish raiders," scoffed Torgerd. "Let's be away while these fiends are occupied."

Torgerd made to move off into the thickets and bushes, but Lorelei remained still, and a curious look came into her eyes. Without comment, she dropped her bag and pulled off her cloak.

"Lorelei," urged Torgerd. "What are you doing? We must leave."

Lorelei drew her sword and tossed the scabbard to the ground, and with swaying hips, like a stalking lion, she approached the enclosure. With one mighty kick, she broke through the wooden plank that held the gate closed. The ogres turned to stare in shock as Lorelei pushed the gate wide and stepped into the pen. The rhino snorted and pulled against its chains. One ogre skipped forward on its crooked legs and snarled with saliva dripping from its yellowed tusk. Long pale arms swung a mighty wooden staff at Lorelei's skull, but her sword, supported by her thick muscles, absorbed the impact, and she darted forward. The ogre screamed and it stumbled backward as its entrails wetted the dirt of the pen. The other three ogres were filled with sudden rage and they charged. Lorelei met them with wrath and power far superior to their own, and her broadsword cut bloody swaths through the lumbering fiends. The ogres fought on, even with severe injuries, too dumb to realize they were already slain. Lorelei's strokes grew more frenzied, and more and more blood pooled in the dirt to become a foul iron-scented mud, and after butchering one ogre and hacking through the neck of another, she kicked the last brute backward. It stumbled but did not fall, and though it was missing a hand and bled from multiple deep cuts, it raised its staff and hissed through blood-stained teeth. However, its battle cry was cut short as an ebony horn erupted from its chest. The ogre was lifted off its feet as it died, and then it was flung violently to the ground. The rhino snorted and stomped in satisfaction.

Quickly, Lorelei found a key among the corpses, and she laid down her sword and cautiously approached the black beast. Her green eyes met its brown ones, and without fear, she carefully unlocked the clasping iron that imprisoned the rhino's legs. She backed away afterward and smiled.

"You are free," she whispered. "You should leave."

The rhino snorted one last time and then it trotted out of the enclosure and was quickly lost to sight, but it could be heard for a few minutes as it trampled through the brush. Torgerd met Lorelei by the edge of the enclosure.

"A mighty risk," she said.

"Worth taking," stated Lorelei. "He did not deserve that enslavement. He was beautiful and strong and deserved to roam as he pleased."

"Aye," said Torgerd with a reluctant nod.

Lorelei grabbed her belongings and the women quickly disappeared among the thickets and headed northwest, while behind them the sky was filling with black smoke and orange flames as the fire grew and began its cleansing conquest of the entire camp.

6. Spriguns

Yellow-green light shined through gloomy purple clouds, and the land grew stranger and eerier the further they traveled on their current course. The thick brush became dotted with large swaths of tall pink grass, the trees became nothing but white dead husks, and fog came upon them at strange times and threatened to bring unseen horrors against them. And though their surroundings grew more alien, it did not disturb Lorelei and she remained focused and calm, but it unnerved Torgerd. The big barbarian cursed under her breath at every swirling cloud and rustling thicket, and she kept her axe in her hands, ready to defend and slay.

Lorelei's mood remained jovial, and she was eager to find the dread pyramid and explore its depths and uncover its treasures and secrets. And she bristled with primal arousal at the thought of testing her strength against the demoness, Kaigora. She would pit the spirit of her Goddess, Kurga, against the will of the Serpent Queen, and only one would emerge victorious. As her eyes scanned the rising fog, her mind wandered and she thought about meeting elves and assessing their prowess in combat, and she longed to squeeze elvish flesh just to see how human-like it was. So excited was she to meet the dangers ahead, that she did not tire as the days wore on, but instead, her strong legs grew stronger and her slaying senses grew sharper.

For six long days they plodded northwest through this creepy expanse, stopping only at night to rest, and lighting no fire to keep their presence concealed. They heard many strange birds and they saw many strange animal tracks, and the days were long and the nights illuminated brightly by an exuberant moon. On the seventh day of travel, they could see a dark line growing in the distance.

"Out there," pointed Lorelei. "A great forest. We are close."

"Aye, but close to what?" growled Torgerd.

"We shall find out," grinned Lorelei with excitement. "Come on."

It took another full day of cautious travel to bring the companions within reach of the forest, and it was indeed great. Its dark trees were tall and thick, with large leaves that cast everything under them into a dark shadow. They camped again, and as the new morning began, they moved slowly towards the forest and paused frequently to scan the trees for signs of movement. A light fog hung over the pink grass that surrounded them, and though it concealed them, they feared it might also conceal the enemy. They felt vulnerable and small, and had they not been experienced travelers and fighters, they may have run towards the trees to escape the gnawing fear that the fog held. Instead, they sunk low into the grass and creeping along slowly brought them to the edge of the trees by mid-morning, and near that great wall of trunks and greenery, they found a strange sight.

In the shadow of the looming forest was a great pool, lined with large white stones whose mineral-infused surface glittered. They approached it and Lorelei leaned over to examine the water. Torgerd quickly reached out a hand and grabbed her shoulder.

"Don't touch the water," said Torgerd as she studied the shadows among the haunted trees. "Elvish water is magic. If you disturb the surface, it will call them to us."

"Perhaps," began Lorelei slowly, "that is exactly what we want."

"What?"

"A guide would be most helpful right now," smirked the berserker. "And what guide could be better than the fiends that live here? I am tired of skulking. Let's find a direct route to our destination. I have demi-gods to slay and treasure to claim. I will give both these gifts of glory to Kurga."

A warm breeze suddenly swirled around the women, and Lorelei smiled cunningly as it tossed her hair and stroked her nipples. Torgerd thought, for a moment at least, that she heard laughter in that strange wind, and though it pleased Lorelei, it unnerved her. It dissipated quickly and the two warriors crouched low.

"You think you can bargain with these sprites?" asked Torgerd.

"I can be persuasive, when need be," said Lorelei.

Torgerd shrugged her broad shoulders while Lorelei studied their surroundings.

"Do you see that thick patch of tall grass and brambles over there?" pointed Lorelei. "Hide there while I call these elves to me."

Torgerd hid herself well, and once that was done, Lorelei dropped her bag and removed her clothes. She paused and thought about what enchantments might be on the water and if they would bewitch her. Finally, she shook away her hesitancy and stepped into the pool. It was cool and refreshing and sent a buzz of excitement through her strong limbs. It was not deep and it was lined with smooth rocks that felt good under her feet. She crouched and ducked under the water and then splashed about a bit, and waited for her prey.

After only a few minutes of waiting, Lorelei smiled as a dozen or so shapes trotted out of the forest gloom. The elves' skin was a sickly pale green color, and over it, they wore bright and garish pants and vests embroidered with vines and strange markings. Some of them were shirtless, including some females, but all were armed with swords slung at their hips in jeweled scabbards. They were thin but well-muscled. Their dark hair was braided, and though their narrow faces were human-like, their ears were pointed and long. They studied Lorelei with dark eyes and hooted to each other in some mysterious language until one shirtless elf stepped forward. He was taller than the others and he licked his lips as he studied Lorelei.

"Do I see a human trespassing in our pool," he sneered. "We did not give you leave to soak in our crystal waters, pale-skinned mongrel."

"I didn't know it belonged to you," said Lorelei apologetically. "I was hot and dusty from traveling, and it looked so refreshing."

"There is a price to pay for stepping into that water," said the elf with a smirk.

"Oh, whatever it is, I will gladly pay it," cooed Lorelei eagerly.

"Hahaha," laughed the elf, and his fellows joined with their guffaws. "A rare prize indeed has found its way to our land. We will be gentle in our sport, Lady, but it will last long. Elves do not tire easily, unlike human scum."

Lorelei stood upright in the pool and the water barely reached above her belly button. The cool liquid ran down her strong arms and her powerful stomach, and her nipples stood erect in the breeze. She climbed from the pool and took a few steps toward the elves. Her powerful thighs shook and flexed and the water clung to the glistening patch of hair above her womanhood. She smiled and shook some damp strands out of her face and she eyed the elves coyly. She took a wide stance and her toes gripped the soft grass and she began to masturbate with one hand, and with the other, she motioned the elves forward. The elves licked their lips and fondled their crotches, and many began to pull off their clothes and drop their weapons in anticipation of a lustful orgy.

"Claim your prize," said Lorelei, and she bit her pouting lip.

This was too much for the lead elf and he strode forward confidently and he firmly gripped Lorelei's heaving breasts. Lorelei played along and grabbed his pounding erection through his silk breeches. The elf moaned as she gave a gentle tug. But then the atmosphere turned to one of menace, and the air grew stagnant, and at that moment several things happened in quick succession. Lorelei's hand became a crushing vice on the elf's groin, and then her fist struck his face with a wet crunch that sent the elf's head backward with blood spraying from a crushed nose. He cursed and clawed at her gripping hand and screamed for his fellows to aid him, but he could not pull away as Lorelei's powerful grasp crushed his privates. The other elves reacted much too slowly and Lorelei grabbed the elf's forgotten short sword and pulled it from its jeweled scabbard, and she set to work with quick murderous strokes that hacked into his lean flesh. His thin neck split apart easily and the decapitated stump gushed blood onto Lorelei's face and body, and then the elf's shoulder and sternum were torn asunder followed in the next stroke by his stomach, and when she finally released the body, it fell into a pile of its own organs and shattered bones.

The other elves were in complete shock by the slaughter before them, but a few began to grab weapons off the ground and charge forward, ignoring their own nakedness. Lorelei jumped over the first corpse to meet the onrushing assault, and her thick muscles rippled under the glistening red gore that adorned them. Like a crimson demon from the hellish labyrinths of Luxor, she hissed and spat, and her green eyes glowed with terrible majesty. She ducked the first elf's attack and cut through both his spindly legs. As he toppled with a grunt she was up and onto the next elf whom she speared with her sword until the hilt struck the she-elf's pale green flesh. The elf gurgled up a fountain of blood while she wailed, and Lorelei shoved the body and sword into the other onrushing elves, forcing them to scatter. Then she turned around and dropped a crushing knee onto the throat of the squirming legless elf, quickly grabbed his sword from the ground, and pounced back into the fray.

The muscles on her hard body stretched and flexed and exploded with energy as she danced about like a mad butcher, cleaving meat with psychotic joy. Her sword cut great gashes across elvish bodies, sending more and more blood and gore onto the ground and into the air as the remaining elves tried to regroup and encircle their enemy. One elf died with her skull cut in half, another with his chest split open, a third with great cuts across his stomach and throat, and two more were gruesomely hacked nearly in half, their bodies spilling entrails onto the other corpses that littered the ground.

Lorelei howled like a banshee and ripped her sword free from the body of her latest victim, and then she spun about in a precise arc that brought her dripping blade down and through the upper arm of a particularly broad elf. Her sword gashed through his abdomen and he fell to the ground with a yell and grabbed at his mutilated stomach with his remaining hand. Lorelei jumped forward and hugged him close to her body so that his face pressed into her belly button. She yanked his head backward, and as he looked into her fiery green eyes, she slowly plunged her sword through his neck and down into his chest cavity. Blood gushed onto her chiseled muscles and ran thickly into her pubic hair, and it cascaded down over her labia. She shoved the corpse away and her body shook with an inner rage born from the abhorrent passions of her grim elder Gods, and with a soft laugh, she inhaled the hellish musk that emanated from her orgy of slaughter.

The last four elves stayed back and their eyes were filled with shock, fear, and a gruesome fascination. Lorelei wiped a hand across the blood that dripped from her breasts and neck, leaving a ghastly smear across her skull tattoos. She licked the blood from her hand and growled at the elves before her.

"She's a demon," said one she-elf with a tall black mohawk.

"A feral God maybe, or a were-beast," said another.

"Kill her quick," said a third, "before she calls more demons to us. Rush her together!"

Three of the elves cautiously closed in and Lorelei went to charge, but her bare toes slipped in the grass, which had become a slick blood-soaked mat. She flailed for a moment and struggled to find purchase amidst the entrails and gore, and as the elves closed in fast, it seemed that the violence she wrought would finally lead to her death. But it was not to happen, and as the closest elf raised her sword high, a thrown dagger struck her in the neck. She dropped the sword and grabbed at the dagger handle and fell spitting up blood. With shouts and curses, the other two elves turned their attention toward the charging red-haired barbarian on their flank. Torgerd's powerful strokes cut through elvish weapons and

75

bodies with ease, and two more corpses joined the ghastly mounds that stretched out before the crystal pool.

Just then a new war party of elvish warriors rushed forward from the forests, called to the pond by the dying screams of their kin. Lorelei crouched and grabbed two swords in her blood-drenched hands, and Torgerd took a step forward and snarled.

Suddenly, a pounding thunder rippled through the ground and caught all the combatants unaware, and a great and powerful snorting was heard, and it was like a battle cry. The surprised shouts of the elves quickly died as a giant black rhino stampeded into their ranks. Bodies were turned to pulp and rent apart under its feet, and its massive horned head stabbed and thrashed about with such force that more than one elf was torn in half. The slaughter was so fast and complete, that in a matter of seconds, the war party was reduced to nothing but dead flesh, which the rhino continued to trample with unbridled glee.

The last elf's naked body trembled with fear and she ran a shaking hand through her ebony mohawk, and when Lorelei's emerald eyes met her own, she lost all her nerve and she dropped her weapon and tried to flee. But she was much too slow and Lorelei tackled her hard and pinned her down. A vicious punch from Lorelei's strong right arm stunned the elf and kept her still. Torgerd stood back and stabbed a few of the elf corpses to make sure they were fully dead, but mostly she wanted to stay away from Lorelei until her battle urges subsided.

Meanwhile, Lorelei pressed the elf's battered face into the turf, and she ground her pelvis against the elf's exposed buttocks to massage her blood-soaked lips as the heat of the massacre had aroused a powerful and ghastly lust in her loins. She humped and raged and orgasmed, and then continued her debauched gyrations with increased fervor amidst groans of hedonistic pleasure. And in the throes of her degenerate ecstasy, while her lecherous ejaculate mixed with the blood of the slaughtered, she heard wild laughter from some otherworldly realm of madness, and it shook her soul and filled her limbs with power and an eagerness to slay again.

Lorelei's depravity sent shivers through Torgerd's strong frame, but she knew that she could not intervene unless she wished to court the unpredictable wrath of the berserker. With a violent grunt, Lorelei pulled the elf's head back by the hair, and then she slowly licked the elf's pointed ear, causing her to squirm. But the weight of Lorelei's iron body kept her trapped and she whimpered as blood-soaked hands gripped her neck and began to squeeze. The murder lust was upon Lorelei, and she longed to feel cracking bones in her hands, but from deep in her subconscious a voice began to assert itself. And slowly, with deep panting breaths, Lorelei calmed her rage and released her death grip from the elf's neck.

The elf wheezed and coughed, and Lorelei leaned in close and motioned Torgerd forward with a side nod. She glanced at the nearby rhino. He snorted at her and his brown eyes watched intently while blood glistened on his black horn. She smiled and turned back to her prone captive.

"Do you wish to live?" Lorelei hissed.

"Aye," said the elf with a trembling voice.

"What is your name?" asked Torgerd.

After a moment's hesitation, she answered, "Valka."

"Are there more of your comrades lurking about, Valka?" asked Lorelei.

"N-no," said Valka. "None within earshot. A-are y-you a demon?" she stammered.

Lorelei shared an amused smile with Torgerd before turning her attention back to the elf.

"You have more than met your match with us," said Lorelei. "Remember that, and we will not end your life. You will take us to the pyramid of Kaigora."

"Ohhhh, cursed Graza," wailed Valka. "I serve the Queen, but I will not go near that hellish temple. The horror of it will blast your mind and send you mad. All who enter her realm die; elf, dwarf, demon, or human, it matters little. All share the same fate."

"Hmph," grunted Lorelei. "Speak not of madness and fear, for they have no claim on our souls. We will meet Kaigora's terror with steel."

"You cannot face the Queen and live," said Valka. "It's impossible."

"That is the price we offer," said Torgerd as she tapped Valka's cheek with her sword tip. "That is the price of your life. If you will not guide us to the pyramid, then we have no use for you. Die now, or aid us and live. What say you?"

The Elf thought hard for a few pained minutes. "Agreed," she whimpered.

Lorelei released her and stood up. She turned, and with confident slow steps, she approached the hulking rhino. She ran a hand over his bloody horn and then she caressed his cheek and looked into his brown eyes. She saw a kindred spirit there, and the berserker and the beast stood in silence for a long while, the blood drying on their skin as their souls found comfort in each other's presence.

"What is your name?" asked Lorelei.

The rhino rumbled and snorted.

"I will call you Woden," said Lorelei. "After the god of waves, worshiped, but also feared, in my homeland. Waves of power and beauty that crush ships and carve rocks with a relentless spirit. Does that suit you, Woden?"

The rhino stomped his mighty feet and nudged Lorelei's hip joyfully. The berserker kissed his snout and laughed. Then she turned around and approached the seated elf, and she bent down and grabbed Valka's dark hair, and she violently pulled her to her feet. Valka studied the two women with terror in her eyes and her gaze lingered on the blood-covered body of Lorelei, and her flesh trembled. Forcefully, Lorelei grabbed her hand and led her towards the pool, and their naked feet squished and slid in the gore-soaked grass.

"We will bathe quickly," said Lorelei, "and then we will seek the pyramid of horrors."

7. Berserkers

Once again, Lorelei stood in the great cavern inside Horgun's Hill. The braziers burned intensely and their shimmering light clawed at the ancient stone walls and the alcoves stuffed with the detritus of history. The air was unusually tense and warm, and Lorelei paced back and forth in front of the marble statue of Kurga, eager to begin the day's training session. For four years she had slipped away from her home in the early morning hours to come to this hallowed chamber. She had grown tall and lovely, like her sisters before her, but unlike her kin, her wiry soft body had been replaced by hard corded muscles. She relished the physical power she now possessed and she smiled as she flexed and strutted about, enjoying the feel of her muscles as blood pumped into her thick shoulders and powerful arms. She glanced often at the pale smirking face of Kurga, Queen of berserkers, longing to know the secrets of her mind.

Beyond intense physical training, the mysteries of ages long past had been revealed to Lorelei. With Zuda's guidance, she studied the writings of priests, warriors, and even necromancers. She obsessed over maps of the world, ancient and current, and she was now a master of a wide range of weapons and combat styles. Lorelei's sweat and blood stained the stone floor, and she yearned to explore the vast lands beyond the Blue Isle, ready to test her fighting skills on the people and beasts she found there.

A grin spread across her face as her mentor appeared from a large alcove on the far side of the chamber. "Hail, Zuda," she said in her customary greeting. "Kurga protect you."

"And you," he responded somberly.

There was something different in his mood. Zuda was not wearing his gold necklaces, and he made no movements towards the iron weights they used for training, nor did he grab any of the dull weapons they used for combat practice. He stood silent in the middle of the room and stared at her with the braziers flashing eerily across his scarred torso, giving the appearance that tendrils of lightning were shooting across his dark body.

"Do we train today?" asked Lorelei.

"No," said Zuda. "There is no more training. There is only the final test. Today you will be one with Kurga, or you will be dead."

"I am ready," said Lorelei with a surge of excitement racing through her veins. This was unexpected news, but not unwelcome.

"We shall see," growled Zuda. Without removing his hard gaze from Lorelei, he kicked off his boots, and then he removed his crimson pants and tossed them aside. He stretched his naked body and barked suddenly like a wolf. Lorelei flinched at the harshness of the sound and the power it held.

He pointed to Lorelei with a blue fire burning in his eyes. "Remove your clothes and let your flesh breathe," he said. "Let Kurga see you."

Without reply, Lorelei did as she was ordered. Her smooth skin and chiseled muscles glowed like fire in the cavern light and she flicked her long blonde hair towards her back, away from her heaving breasts. She was tall and beautiful and her hard body was filled with the passions of youth. Standing naked in that elder chamber of forbidden knowledge stirred a deep lust inside her, and she could feel the moisture building quickly between her powerful thighs.

"Do you see the skulls of Kurga," said Zuda, and he pointed at the necklace of ancient bones hanging on the pale statue. "Today, one of our heads will join that ring in sacrifice. That is your final test, Lorelei, goatherder. Win in combat against me and give a great sacrifice to her who we hold most dear."

Shock and uncertainty flooded Lorelei's mind and her heart trembled. "Is there no way to avoid this bloodshed?" she pleaded. "Surely two of us traveling this world would serve her better than one. Test me in another manner!"

"There is no other way," said Zuda. "The world has grown too civilized. It can only handle one true disciple of Kurga at a time. One true berserker. One true God-killer. One true agent of Chaos. If I have served my Goddess well, then you will take my place. If not, then I will turn your village to ash and trample what's left into the blood-soaked ground. And then I will search for another disciple."

"Four years," whispered Lorelei, more to herself than to Zuda. "And this is how it ends?"

"Woof," he barked, and his eyes flashed like a mad beast. "Die or be reborn!"

Zuda stalked forward with menace in his step and ferocity surging through his iron limbs. His thick muscles rippled with violent intent and he barked and slapped his chest. Lorelei tried to steel her heart as he came and she gave a quick shake of her body to prepare, then he was upon her.

Lorelei attacked first and stepped toward him and swung her fist, but Zuda was faster, and his iron knuckles battered her jaw and she crumpled to the floor in a daze. Before she could regain her bearing, a bright pain coursed through her as Zuda savagely grabbed her breast. Her scream was cut short as another punch caused the world to momentarily go black. She came too quickly and spit blood onto the stone floor. Zuda loomed over her, a great shadow of death in the form of her beloved mentor. He reached for her again and she kicked upward into his stomach, sending him back several paces. She hopped to her feet and glared at the red finger marks on her breast.

"Your enemies will look on your body and see vulnerability," growled Zuda. "They will see weakness to exploit. You must use their ignorance as a weapon, like any other. They know nothing of Kurga. You will teach them! To know Kurga is to be invincible! Her protection is the only cloak you need in battle! No armor or sorcery will ever serve you better. Fight in your true flesh and honor her, and you will find victory.

Feel her presence as the wind brushes your skin and deliver her glory upon those that oppose you! Woof!"

Zuda pounced again and he easily passed under Lorelei's meager counterattack. His fists rained destruction upon her stomach and head, and as she reeled, his elbow crushed her face. Her body fell away from him, but he caught her by her long hair and tugged it viciously to keep her close. She coughed blood and struck at his iron arm while his free hand continued to pummel her body. Zuda's knee brutalized her stomach, and her ribs began to crack under the assault. His fists slammed into her breasts and then into her temple, and she would have collapsed again if he had let her. He tugged hard on her hair and then, with a choking grasp on her neck, he held her upright and looked into her stunned eyes.

"Fight," he barked. "Is this how you would die, young fool? A pitiful woman playing at being a warrior? Fight! Kurga gave you a strong body, but where is the spirit!?"

A quick pivot and Zuda threw Lorelei face down onto the floor. He quickly landed on top of her and bent her right arm behind her body. She screamed as he increased the pressure, and he spat on her face and roared like an enraged bear. Images, distorted by pain, flashed in her mind; of her sisters in the fields, of the ocean waves against the shore, of the years she had trained with the man that was now killing her. The pain began to focus her as Zuda's free hand punched her in the side. The dust on the tiles mixed with her blood and saliva and tears, and it became a foul paste that coated her face as Zuda slammed her cheek against it.

"Kurga trusted you, welp!" he roared. "Is this how you repay her? Is this weakness how you repay me?! I have given you everything!"

Zuda twisted her arm more and she fought back with all her strength, hoping her bones would not break under his iron might. "Fight!" he screamed. "Where is the savage inside? Where is the fire I saw in you when we first met? Where is the berserker!? I will slay thee, betrayer, for deceiving me and wasting my knowledge! Find Kurga or die!"

Zuda raged and sprawled upon her and pressed against her flesh, and the fire of his violence aroused him. He rubbed his stiff manhood against her buttocks and then he slipped it between her thighs to rub against her exposed vagina. "Perhaps I should have taught you about the devilry of men," he spat. "Perhaps that is all you're good for? Do you need a lesson before I slay thee?!"

The heat of his penis was like a firebrand to Lorelei's soul, and with sudden power, she freed her arm, bucked him off of her back, and smashed his jaw with a spinning elbow. She followed through with savage punches that broke his nose, snapped his teeth, and shattered a cheekbone. Lorelei stood tall and a red haze swam before her eyes. Rising to his feet, Zuda spit a mouthful of blood and molars into Lorelei's face to blind her, but she struck hard with her eyes closed and her foot crushed his engorged groin. He fell with a moan. Lorelei felt suddenly alive, in a way she had never felt before in her life, and the pain in her body fell away like a shadow meeting the rising sun. She wiped the blood from her eyes and kicked at Zuda's bent head, but he was less incapacitated than he seemed and he caught her leg and twisted his strong body, and Lorelei was thrown to the floor. She quickly rolled away to gain distance and then she got to her feet and eyed Zuda fiercely.

"Now, you are ready," growled Zuda as he stood up. "Now, we begin!"

Zuda grabbed a sharp sword from a nearby alcove, and Lorelei backed up and did the same, grabbing a brutal mace with a spiked ball at the end of its wooden shaft. Without words, they pounced at one another, spit and blood littering the floor while their murderous blows clashed. They were like rabid bears tearing at one another, seeking blood and death at any cost. Zuda had speed and strength bolstered by decades of fighting experience, but Lorelei matched his speed and surpassed him in ferocity, and she kept his sword at bay with her death cudgel. They seemed like equals for several violent minutes, but that changed when Zuda's flashing steel cut Lorelei's shoulder. She ignored the pain and struck back, but the sword cut again, through her thigh. She stumbled, and a moment of panic gripped her guts as burning sweat and muck dripped into her eyes. Then Zuda's blade bit into her side, not deeply, but it raked against her corded muscles and nicked a rib. Zuda roared sensing victory, but just as his blade slid free of her flesh, Lorelei's mace found a home in his broad chest.

He stumbled with a surprised grunt, and he barked as the weapon was ripped free. Before he could counter, the mace was brutally slammed into his privates. With a scream, he swung his steel, but Lorelei ducked the killing blow, and her mace was savagely torn upwards to gash his stomach and rake his chest before destroying his chin. His iron grip faltered and he dropped his sword, and he fell to a knee. Zuda's body was a wreck, awash with butchery. Blood gushed from the deep lacerations in his stomach, from the slashes and holes in his chest, from his mangled face, and it poured amidst the dangling gore that was once his groin. With a deep steadying breath, he looked up to see Lorelei's blazing emerald eyes. He was caught by the swirling depths of those mesmerizing orbs as she violently smashed her mace into his stomach with all the power she could muster. And with her victory assured, a terrible and guttural scream erupted from her throat, like a demonic beast newly born, barring its soul with a single primal sound to the world it would soon devour.

She released the handle of the weapon and Zuda fell onto his back, blood seeping from around the iron that remained lodged in his torso. Lorelei picked up his sword and spun it around, enjoying the heft of the blade. Then she knelt by his side and looked with remorse upon the man whom she considered as dear to her as her father. The horror of her actions pressed upon her in the swelling madness of that ancient violent chamber. Her eyes began to water and her limbs shook. Zuda reached out a bloody hand and patted her on the thigh.

"For Kurga, I die," he wheezed. "And for Kurga, you live. You will be greater than all who have come before you. Lord Reh prophesized it, and that is why this temple lives on this island of peace. Kurga was waiting for you." Zuda's trembling hand poked Lorelei above the breast. "You carry her soul, reincarnated for glory and passion, and love of this mortal realm. She lives now, as you live."

Tears fell in rivulets down Lorelei's battered and stained face as she lifted Zuda's sword. "Praise to Kurga," she whispered. A broad smile stretched across Zuda's face and Lorelei swung the blade and hacked through flesh and bone, embedding the steel in the flagstones beneath. Zuda's blood pooled around Lorelei's legs, and in the face of her butchery, she wept for a long while before she was able to gather herself and finish her grisly task.

She took Zuda's head and she laid it at Kurga's feet, and with a hand covered in his blood, she pressed her palm onto the statue's left breast. Then she leaned forward and pressed her trembling lips against the right breast and kissed it fiercely. The ghastly totem dripped down the white stone as Lorelei backed away, and in that terrible moment of abhorrent reverence, Lorelei struggled to wipe the blood and sweat from her eyes, and to her exhausted gaze, it seemed that the statue's grin grew larger and more pronounced.

Lorelei pressed her hand in the puddle of Zuda's blood, and then she gripped her own left breast in mimicry of Kurga's new crimson marking. And breathing in the heavy miasma of fresh death, she felt a presence within her, a spirit, arisen and reborn. She took a confident stance and bowed her head. "Hail, Kurga," she whispered with halting breaths. "I serve thee now and forever. Through my limbs, you live again. I hope I will not disappoint thee."

Ignoring her pain, Lorelei lifted Zuda's headless body, and under the streams of blood which ran from the corpse down her naked muscles, she carried it out of the cavern and up onto the hilltop. She labored without rest and built a pyre, and as dusk approached, she engulfed it in flames, and for generations, the people of the Blue Isle would talk about the demonic fire that they witnessed from afar on that night. And as the pyre raged, Lorelei lay nearby in the warm grass, her nudity marred by bruises and cuts, caked in dried blood and muck. And before sleep took her, she would swear that she saw a face in the flames; Lord Reh come to claim a proud warrior's soul.

Dead branches cracked and moaned amid the soft buzzing of insects, and a deep shadow fell over the sleeping form of Lorelei. Her emerald eyes opened swiftly and her strong hand thrust a dagger upward with murderous intent. Torgerd caught her wrist just before the dagger could sink into her thick neck. Lorelei grabbed Torgerd's hair with her free hand, and she gritted her teeth as she pushed harder, seeking death and blood. Torgerd resisted with all her might, and her muscles strained to hold the berserker at bay. Nearly a minute passed in this tense standoff before the red haze cleared from Lorelei's vision, and her taut arms began to relax.

"Torgerd," whispered Lorelei as she lowered her dagger and released her friend's hair.

"It's time, Lorelei," said Torgerd calmly. "Valka has found the path that will take us to the pyramid. Doom calls us home."

Lorelei rose and quickly rolled up her blanket and prepared to travel. The forest trees towered overhead and blotted out the sun. The canopy above cast the underbrush in hues of purple and blue and dark green. The forest felt cluttered, untamed, and strangely humid. Nearby, the great black rhino, Woden, munched on sweet ferns and listened intently for approaching enemies. Valka the elf stood upon a green mossy trail that was barely discernable from the rest of the forest.

"This path will lead us to Kaigora," whispered Valka. "We can still turn back if you wish. Harmless though it looks, this trail of moss ends in death."

"Lead on," said Lorelei without hesitation.

Valka sighed and took the path with Torgerd close on her heels. Lorelei paused and rubbed Woden behind one of his large ears.

"Glory awaits," she whispered to the beast with a sly smile.

Woden tossed his head and rumbled in acknowledgment. Then Lorelei took the path and the rhino lumbered after her. For several hours they moved silently through the forest, and the longer they stayed on the mossy path, the fewer insects they heard and fewer birds did they see, until they reached a point where they were sure they were utterly alone. It was unnatural and unnerving, and Lorelei's skin prickled at the dread stillness of the vast forest around them. She left Woden's side and walked forward to speak with the elf.

"How much further?" asked Lorelei.

"We will be there soon," said Valka despondently.

Lorelei grunted her approval and began to eat some salted jerky from her pack. She tossed an extra piece to Torgerd who devoured it quickly.

"Why do this?" asked Valka cautiously.

"I need a reason to kill monsters?" responded Lorelei after swallowing her food.

Valka shook her head. "You will not kill the Serpent Queen. She is eternal. A force of nature. She is as unkillable as the wind."

"Then I need a reason to kill myself, is that it?" smirked Lorelei.

"You could live your life without ever coming within a hundred leagues of this place," hissed Valka. "Kaigora would never seek you out, so why do you seek her?"

"Should a healthy woman knowingly sleep next to a room with plague-ridden corpses and hope that she remains untouched? Or should that woman burn the house down and kill the sickness before it infects her and those she cares for?"

"So, you come to protect humanity? You?! I say your words are false. You are a slayer, yes? Why would you die for the human masses? I bet you have killed many men with your own hands."

"Men and women, yes, by the dozens," cooed Lorelei menacingly and without a hint of remorse. "And that number will stretch into the hundreds, maybe more, before my blood lust is quenched, if it ever can be."

"Then why?" asked Valka as she pushed past a low-hanging tree branch.

"My Goddess is curious. She craves knowledge and excitement. I seek the demons of this world for her, to see and learn their mysteries, and then to slay them if I can. I roam the land according to my own whims while I feed Kurga the passions of life. Does that answer asway you, Elf? I have come to stand before Kaigora, and with my blade, I'll show the Serpent Queen that she is nothing compared to the mortal flesh of Kurga's daughter."

"So, you do not come for treasure," said Valka reflectively. "Then you are different than all the fools who have come before."

"Wrong," laughed Lorelei. "I do come for treasure, or at least, treasure is an added incentive. There is one treasure in particular that I seek. An iron object more valuable to me than any gem. Ancient rumors place it within Kaigora's vast halls."

"What is this object of iron?" asked Valka dubiously. "Surely it is the least precious item in a pyramid overflowing with gold and rare stones."

"It is something that was stolen before Thordamis sunk beneath the ocean, and before the towers of Greko burned in the black flames of the Necro Witches. It is a crown, forged by nameless demigods of rage and hate. It was bequeathed to me in blood, and I have come to claim it."

Valka fell silent as a shiver ran up her spine. She wanted to run, but there was nowhere to go. She was caught in a web of madness and she could see no scenario where they might survive. With her head downtrodden she trudged along for another hour until a familiar cloying scent tickled her nose. She held up a hand and faced the others. With dread gripping her heart she whispered, "We are here."

8. Dungeon Crawl

Menace hung in the air, clinging to a scent that was both sweet and abhorrent. It assaulted their nostrils and wormed its way into their bodies like a vicious parasite, and no amount of snorting could remove it. The lurid stench excited their hedonistic souls, but it also made their limbs feel sluggish like they were suddenly carrying great burdens. Lorelei's tongue felt numb and her nipples grew hard like stones. She looked at Torgerd, and by the expression of dread she bore, she knew that her red-headed companion was also feeling the effects of the swirling miasma. Torgerd's eyes met hers and a moment of doubt crossed them. A silent understanding passed between them; this was their last chance to turn back. For an instant Lorelei faltered and she nearly capitulated to Torgerd's silent plea, thinking it better to live a long life among men than it was to die horribly in an ancient tomb of demons. But the moment passed quickly and Lorelei snarled as she gripped the handle of her sword. Vapors, no matter how noxious or cloying, would not deter her from her task.

Torgerd knew that the berserker would not retreat, and thus, neither could she. A small chuckle escaped her throat and she nodded to Lorelei, signaling that she would also not be deterred by the sorcerous miasma. Together, they crept forward, crawling on their stomachs until they reached a point where the mossy path descended out of view into some sort of clearing. Cautiously, they looked over a mass of gnarled tree roots to finally gaze upon the destination they sought.

The trees before them gave way and the land sloped down into a deep bowl-like impression, and standing in the middle, in a wide meadow of multi-colored moss, was a massive and ghastly pyramid. It was made of great stones, cyclopean in size and green in color, like emeralds but veined with sickly streaks of yellow and black. Much of the smooth surface was covered in a shimmering slime that shifted between hues of pink, blue, and green as it stretched across the stones like a labyrinthine web of madness. High up on the pyramid, uneven dark holes gaped like caves, and from their blackness crept the foul miasma in shimmering waves to fill the meadow and the surrounding forest. One look at the pyramid told Lorelei a sobering truth. This was a place of gods and demons. A place not meant for humans, no matter how bold. Even Valka blanched under the weight of terror brought on by the legendary palace of the Serpent Queen. Tears pooled in her elven eyes and she knew that she beheld the location of her own cruel demise.

For a moment the miasma wafted thickly into their faces and a strange vision swam before Lorelei's burning eyes. She saw an army of elves laboring in a clearing much like this one but with a more wholesome aspect. And walking among the elves was a great elf maiden, taller than all the rest, with eyes that gleamed like crystals and beautiful auburn hair blowing in the wind. While the other elves toiled as they pulled stone blocks on sleds, the maiden single-handedly lifted a large block and stacked it onto the foundation stones that were already in place. She leapt upon the green stones and laughed wildly as she lifted a black snake and let it curl around her long slender neck. Lorelei shook her head and the vision cleared, and she knew with certainty that she had just seen Kaigora the Serpent Queen, in the halcyon days when this foul pyramid had been given life. It was a vision into a past that was now buried by the unassailable weight of history and forgetfulness.

Looking at the structure again, it was hard to believe that elvish hands, no matter how skilled or strong, could have built it. It was sunk into the great meadow as if the very earth was cowed by the weight of its putridness. It was a fortress of terror, a citadel of demonic pleasure, an obscene monument from an older time when madness ruled the world.

At the base of the pyramid, a single crooked entrance glared at them, like a scar cut through rotten flesh. The entrance held no gate or portcullis, and it was pitted and marked from centuries of erosion. A swirling whistle trickled out of the insidious opening, followed by two guards that strutted awkwardly on gangly limbs, unaware of the ghastliness of their forms. They walked on two legs like men, but they were not men. Their upper bodies were built of thick slabs of muscle, and their arms were longer than a man's and their feet were wider and their toes ended in claws. And sitting atop sinuous thick necks were heads akin to monstrous lizards. Drool dangled from their long lips and forked tongues repeatedly dashed forward to taste the scents in the air. The lizard men carried long crude blades and they were naked. Lorelei gaped for a moment at the size and girth of the creatures' penises, but she was not amused or aroused by what she saw. Instead, she grimaced as a slaying lust tingled up her spine and crept down her arms.

The miasma still pressed on her limbs and they felt sluggish. She didn't know if she could reach the lizard men before they could raise an alarm. She needed to shock them and close the distance quickly. Quietly, she pulled back until she stood in front of the massive horned head of Woden. The great rhino's black hide melted into the deep forest shadows, and Lorelei could feel the unbridled power that emanated from his stoic posture. She stroked his cheek and kissed his great horn.

"The time has come to show courage in the face of madness," said Lorelei. "Will you fight with me, Woden? Shall we break the shackles of this foul smoke and crush all the demons we can find?"

Woden shook his head and his lips tugged on her shirt. Lorelei smiled and she scratched Woden's ear. Then she leaped onto his broad back like a panther leaping into a tree.

Torgerd grabbed Valka and rolled them both out of the way as Woden's feet pounded the earth, nearly crushing them in his excitement. They recovered in time to witness the shock that glazed over the reptilian eyes of the guards as the massive rhino charged into the meadow and bore down on them from the slope. Lorelei raised her sword high as they approached the first lizard man and she snarled as it raised its sword with a quick clap of its long snout. But the lizard was too slow, and as it moved to avoid the charging beast, Lorelei's blade sheared through its scaly head. The lizard's body spun about and collapsed into a pile with blood and gore tumbling from its wound. The second lizard man tried to dodge Woden, but it was caught by his thrashing head and tossed twenty yards. The sound of snapping bones rang in the silent glade as the lizard landed, and Lorelei jumped from the rhino's back and charged her fallen foe. The lizard man propped itself on one arm and swung its rusty blade at Lorelei, hoping to cut her in half. She was prepared for this feeble strike and she leapt over the lizard's blade and landed with a downward stroke that severed its sword arm. Blood shot from the wound but the lizard ignored its butchered flesh and it threw itself into Lorelei's legs, knocking her to the ground.

The lizard man quickly pulled its mass on top of Lorelei, even as she repeatedly punched it in the head. Lorelei adjusted her grip on her sword and stabbed the blade through the lizard's sinuous neck. Inhuman reptilian eyes glared at her and a forked tongue slithered forward and groped her lips. Lorelei glanced down between their struggling bodies, and she saw the fiend's thick member spasm just before it began to urinate on her legs. With great effort, she pushed her blade upward and nearly severed the neck completely. The reptile's blood gushed forth as she rolled over to dump its lifeless body into the moss.

Valka and Torgerd came to her side quickly and studied the dead lizard man.

"What blasphemous beast is this?" spat Torgerd.

"They are called goahgs," shivered Valka. "The unbreakable servants of Kaigora, protectors of the pyramid, hunters and slavers, and much worse."

"These two broke easily enough," snorted Lorelei. "But they do not seem to feel pain. In the corridors of the pyramid, they will be deadly."

Torgerd and Lorelei began to prepare in earnest now, and they left behind everything that could not be used to slay or maim. They tucked daggers into their belts and boots, lashed small torches to their sides, and they rolled their shoulders, and stretched their muscles.

When she was ready, Lorelei approached Woden. She touched heads with the rhino and then looked him in the eye. "This is where you must stay," she said. "It will be hard for you to move inside this foul catacomb. You will be too vulnerable."

Woden shook his head and stomped his feet, unwilling to leave Lorelei's side.

"I know," she said soothingly. "But you must do something for me. You must be a rear guard so that no enemies enter behind us and catch us unaware. Guard this meadow and crush all who enter it, be they elf, goahg, or lost traveler. Can you do that for me?"

Woden stood silent for a minute and then he dipped his head and pushed against Lorelei's thighs. She quickly kissed the rhino's forehead and then she joined her companions near the pyramid's doorway.

They stood for many long minutes, looking into the blackness of the tunnel beyond, their minds racing with thoughts of the horrors they would find. Fighting back the temporary paralysis, Lorelei smirked and spat on the ground. She shook out her powerful shoulders one last time and readied herself. Torgerd tightened her belt and then hefted her battle axe.

Lorelei began to unbutton her shirt as her battle lust grew, but she suddenly stopped. The growing stench of the miasma made her skin prickle with goosebumps and she was suddenly very uncomfortable with the idea of entering the mysterious catacombs without layers of clothing to protect her from the grime and grotesqueries that lay ahead. She glared at the trembling slime that throbbed and moved through the cracks of the pyramid's stone surface like a living thing. She shuddered and her hands fell to her sides. Torgerd noticed her hesitancy and without a word, she stepped forward to lead the way into the yawning doorway of terror. Lorelei grabbed Torgerd's arm and stopped her.

"You don't have to go," said Lorelei with sudden concern. "You have done enough to aid me. Remain with Woden as a rear guard. You need not expose your soul to the demons within."

"You took my life in fair combat, as I sought to take yours," began Torgerd. "And then you returned it to me, in an act of generosity that I can never match. And so, at the very doorstep of Hel, I must confess my intentions. I do not enter seeking recompense for your actions, nor do I seek a glorious second death. I enter because I must. Because the monster within must be slain and I deem that we have the might to do so. That means we must try or we will forever be haunted by our own cowardice, and we will fade and die without honor. I enter not because of what I owe to you, but because we are sisters. And I will never abandon my sister no matter how much fear grips my heart."

Lorelei looked deeply into Torgerd's eyes for a long moment, and then she smiled. "Aye, sister," she said. "Let us stalk these demons and paint their Hel with their own blood. Let us soothe the serpent with cold steel, and we shall fight and die for ourselves, and no others."

"Aye," replied Torgerd with a broad smile that lightened the icy grip in her chest.

Without another word, Lorelei hoisted her sword and the three companions stepped into the dark maw, Torgerd in the lead and Lorelei at the rear.

Inside the pyramid, the companions were greeted by a winding near-maze of corridors, rooms, and hidden alcoves. Sometimes the path was straight, and sometimes curved, but the same dread and menace hung in the fetid air. The catacombs were filthy, with slime-covered walls and rats infesting every nook and corner. Scraps of bone were strewn about, the stones were stained with crimson blotches, and the air was extremely warm and humid. Venka was little help, as she had never entered the pyramid, knowing that if she had, she would never have left it alive. Occasionally, they would hear clawed feet, and they would duck into a side room or passage until silence again reigned. The disorienting and cluttered layout made it easy to avoid enemies and remain unseen.

But sometimes, glittering masses would gibber at them from some room or hole in a wall, and quivering slime-like arms would stretch forth in mockery of a human body. In these moments they ran, preferring to face flesh and blood enemies than to encounter the more horrific and insane denizens of the pyramid.

The tunnels were not lit by torches, but the mold that grew thickly on the walls glowed and provided enough light for the companions to see without aid. Lorelei began to take notice of the intricate carvings that ran across the tops of the walls near the vaulted ceilings. An elven face of stunning beauty protruded in relief every twenty feet or so. Lorelei recognized the face of the Serpent Queen from her recent vision, and seeing the face carved in stone was eerie and unnerving. Delicately carved freezes stretched between each protruding face, showing scenes of elves mingling with dwarves, fairies, and strange unidentifiable creatures. Scenes of wars and battles long forgotten were mixed with bold erotic stories, and some depictions were so odd that Lorelei deemed they must be mythological. Sometimes the carvings were eroded or covered in mold, but they stretched on down every corridor, an unbreaking history of the ancient elves who built this phantasmagorical structure.

As they moved further into the pyramid, the freezes began to show more and more serpents mingling with the elves, and the protruding faces of Kaigora began to change. It was almost imperceivable at first, but it became more pronounced until a point where the face, and all subsequent faces, had been crudely smashed or carved away. Lorelei was unnerved by the faces, but she was disturbed even more by their sudden disappearance and what that forbade.

Torgerd hissed and waved an arm, and the companions ducked into a small room. Moments later a group of large goahgs marched passed in double file lines. They wore long golden cloaks over their bodies, with high collars, and between them walked dark-skinned men with hands tied and bound. Venka grabbed Lorelei's arm as she was wracked with a bout of fear.

"That is the Swagoab Elite," she said. "They are the strongest of the goahgs. If you see the golden cloaks you must run, or you will suffer a fate worse than death. We must flee."

"We are not fleeing," spat Lorelei.

Torgerd griped Venka's shoulder hard to hold her in place while Lorelei peered into the corridor.

"It's clear," said Lorelei, "Let's keep moving."

A few minutes later, the sounds of heavy breathing and grunting began to echo down the stone corridors, and after crossing through some connected rooms, Torgerd and Lorelei peaked through a tattered cloth that covered a hidden alcove, and their eyes widened in shock. The next room was a broad hall full of elves. But these elves were not armed, nor were they clothed. They writhed on the grimy stone floor in tangled masses, fornicating like made beasts, with wild bloodshot eyes and drooling mouths. The elves strolled about from one partner to the next without rest, like mindless spell-bound automatons.

"Can we get passed them?" asked Torgerd. "Should we go back and find another passage?"

Lorelei thought for a minute, then she grabbed Venka and shoved her into the room. Venka froze with terror and stood like a statue amid her kin's orgiastic revelry. She looked about frantically, ready to fight or flee, but neither was required. The elves ignored her. Some glanced at her without care and a few reached into her vest to paw at her breasts before turning back to find another partner. After a few minutes, Lorelei and

Torgerd stalked into the room, befuddled. And like Venka, the elves ignored the humans.

Torgerd smirked and slowly picked her way through the throng and headed for the far end of the hall. Lorelei followed, and though it was impossible not to touch any of the elves, she did her best to remain free of their groping and flailing limbs. Eventually, they could see a doorway at the end of the hall, and an escape from the ejaculating masses. They followed whatever path opened and this moved them closer to a wall.

It was here that many elves fornicated standing upright, pressing themselves against the moldy walls. Their bodies began to press tightly against the companions and Lorelei growled and began to elbow the naked forms. One elf became aggressive and grabbed Lorelei's breasts. Her dagger flashed and the elf grunted and fell back against the wall with blood spilling from his stomach. He died silently and fell over into the filth and scurrying rats. His fellows ignored his body and continued with their mindless pleasure-seeking.

"Madness," muttered Lorelei.

Just then a slapping was heard and Lorelei turned as a goahg charged at her, its heavy feet pounding on the stone floor. She dodged as a heavy cleaver whizzed past her face and embedded itself in an elf's chest. Her sword countered and split open the goahgs side. It tumbled to the floor and Lorelei's steel quickly pierced its skull.

Shadows danced on the walls and bodies collided and slid about, and Lorelei could not tell which were threats and which belonged to the ongoing orgy.

"We must get out of this carnal mass," hissed Lorelei as her eyes darted about.

"This way," said Torgerd, and she shoved elves to the side and headed for the nearby doorway.

Once they were free of the sexual madness, they found themselves in a narrow room covered in tapestries with strange writing intertwined with striped serpents. Torgerd spit on the ground, disturbed by the ominous fabrics.

"The language of the ancient serpents," whispered Valka. "The language of death."

"There are no serpent gods here," sneered Lorelei. "Only the rotting, putrid reek of demons."

A pair of female elves stumbled into the room, their faces locked together and their probing hands griping each other between the thighs. Lorelei could no longer trust the mindlessness of these slaves to debauchery, and she sprung forward and her sword cut a powerful arc that beheaded both figures. They tumbled in a mass of spouting gore, and in that instant several goahgs entered the room and attacked ferociously.

Torgerd shoved Valka to the ground and charged forward to meet the first goahg. It was fast and lithe and it dodged her axe and its claws cut her side, and then its jaws bit into her arm. Her axe crashed down onto its back, severing the spine and making the goahg go limp, but its jaws still clamped on her arm. Valka jumped forward and she grabbed a dagger from Torgerd's belt and she cut deep into the sinews of the lizard's neck. The jaws opened and the dead goahg fell forward, leaving Torgerd and Valka in a standoff, facing each other with bloody weapons. The tension lasted for only a moment, as Valka handed the dagger back to Torgerd, who grunted her approval.

Lorelei pulled her sword free from another dead goahg. Her lip now bled from being head-butted in the face by the lizard man, but other than that, she was unscathed.

"We move," she said sharply, and she took the lead and quickly scurried through another broad hall and into a curving corridor. This led to a large ornate doorway cut from white marble, embedded with rubies. Extraordinary heat radiated out of the doorway along with a substantial glow of golden light. Tears fell from Valka's eyes and Torgerd smirked at Lorelei. The berserker smiled back.

Ignoring their minor wounds, they crept into the next room and found themselves in a wide cloister surrounding a vast chamber. Gold and gems were piled high in a haphazard fashion covering much of the floor and leaving only small walking paths through the wide spaces, like forest trails through thick underbrush. The magnitude of the treasure before them stunned their minds and made them temporarily forget their purpose. It was wealth beyond comprehension.

The heat in the room was oppressive and it pressed on their shoulders and made their minds sag from sudden exhaustion. Their shirts and pants were quickly soaked through with sweat, and it burned their eyes fiercely and made their palms slick against the shafts of their weapons. The stench in the room was also overpowering and complex, threatening to send them into a spiraling madness. Yet, within its strange essence, the smell of honey came to the forefront and it teased their sweaty lips and their blasted senses. For a moment, Lorelei rubbed at her crotch uncontrollably, and then she nearly collapsed as a powerful and deep orgasm flooded her loins. Rapid breaths kept her from screaming out in pleasure as her legs shook and her muscles spasmed. When it was over, she felt another sudden upwelling of erotic desire building, but she fought the urges back, and with gritted teeth and clenched fists she cautiously stalked forward, using the towering mounds of treasure as cover.

They slunk around the hill-like masses of gold like mice in a grain bin until they found a clump of massive gem-filled vases set in a tight semicircle. From this well-concealed perch, Lorelei and Torgerd peeked into the heart of the chamber and saw the horror which they sought. In the center of that great room, on a raised dais covered with large pillows, lounged Kaigora the Serpent Queen.

9. Serpent Queen

Lorelei wiped the burning sweat from her eyes as she grappled with what she saw. Her chest tightened and her heart pounded rapidly as fear flooded her body from the most primal parts of her brain. The enormity of her foolishness came crashing down upon her, and the failure of her quest became an insurmountable finality. Kaigora's form was vast and imposing, and it made Lorelei feel weak and impotent. For here was a demon goddess of such vibrance, luridness, and horrifically impossible strength, that simply looking upon her could crush one's soul. An aura of violence and dread radiated from her figure in palpable waves that made Lorelei quail and grip her pounding chest. And at the same time, the serpent stench clawed at her mind, drool fell from her quivering lips, her legs wobbled with weakness, and her loins ached. Kaigora was a creature of flesh and blood, but also one empowered by a terrible spirit of malice and lust that smote all living beings with the madness of an elder god unrestrained.

The Queen's naked body was human in form with two arms and two long legs, but they were built from muscles of such a staggering size that Lorelei's own muscularity now seemed laughable and frail in comparison. Kaigora reclined brazenly on a mountain of pillows, yet her muscles bulged outward in extreme proportions, covered in veins and striations, and they exuded power beyond belief. The flesh of her body was pale like a pampered merchant's wife, except for her forearms and hands which were covered in black scales that shimmered with blue sparkles as they moved about to caress her full and ample breasts and her boulder-like abdominal muscles. Thin strands of gold webbing, interlaced with diamonds, hung around her neck and teased her breasts, and another band was like a sash around the curves of her hips. And sitting atop her massive shoulders, swaying to and fro, was a great scale-covered neck, and upon that neck was the broad flat head of a great viper. Flecks of blue iridescence shone on the black scales as the serpentine head lolled about, eyes closed, in a trance of its own making. A ruby-red forked tongue occasionally split the smooth lips of the Serpent Queen, tasting the heavy air that was filled with her own overpowering musk.

Surrounding the dais stood many goahgs, male and female, and some were armed with swords and others were armed with cleavers or crossbows. Unlike the Swagoab Elite, these goahgs wore no garments. They were also not affected by the extreme heat and humidity of the chamber, which continued to make Lorelei and Torgerd sweat profusely. The goahgs swayed in unison with their deplorable Queen, attuned to her cyclic rhythms. Suddenly, Kaigora's eyes opened wide and the power of those yellow orbs seemed to shine extra light into the already well-lit chamber, and the gold and gems sparkled brighter and shined their glow back upon her black scales, which now flashed like eldritch bursts of blue lightning on a field of darkness. Kaigora slowly stood up and walked forward upon dainty black-scaled feet and Lorelei guessed that she was easily ten feet tall at the shoulders, and she seemed nearly as wide. The goahgs backed away from the dais and then fell to the floor and laid their lizard heads flat on the hot stones.

Kaigora crouched, gripped her pale knees with scaly hands, and a hiss escaped her throat as her bulbous abdominal muscles clenched fiercely, and the flesh between her legs split wide and a large leathery egg pushed forth and rolled onto the floor, followed by a second.

Torgerd covered her mouth with a shaky hand at the insanity she was witnessing. Lorelei's eyes were wide with dread fascination and she ignored the burning sweat that ran into them in streams.

Kaigora's flesh recovered quickly from the laying, and in only minutes she was restored to a vision of womanhood unmarred. Her scaled head reached down and nudged the two eggs, which immediately began to seethe and rock. The leathery hides stretched and split apart and arms reached upwards into the glowing chamber, followed by lizard-like heads and the snapping of newly birthed jaws. The first young goahg crawled away towards some unknown alcove, but the second, a male, stayed with the Queen. A golden liquid like honey began to drip from her breasts and the goahg leapt forward and hungrily suckled on the demonic nectar. The little goahg flexed its arms as it drank in the serpent's power and its dangling penis became engorged and stiff. The Queen gripped it lovingly and tugged it gently as her lips spread hideously wide and her mouth slowly opened. The goahg remained frozen in primal ecstasy as Kaigora's mouth pressed over its head and down beyond its shoulders. The great serpent's neck stretched upward and its muscles rippled as it pulled the goahg down into Kaigora's stomach. In only a matter of minutes, the Queen had given life and taken it back, in a display of obscenity and debauchery that made the companions nearly retch in their hidden location.

With a herculean effort, Lorelei tore her gaze away from the Queen, and she turned to studying the chamber and planning her attack. There were few, if any, paths where they could sneak up on the demon queen. The center of the chamber was an open space and everything beyond was piled with treasure, blocking all secret approaches towards the raised dais. Scattered about were large braziers heaped with fires that burned so hot that the metal bands around them were bright red. To assault the Queen, they needed to get closer before she saw them, and Lorelei had no idea how they would accomplish this. She debated retreating and waiting to see if Kaigora ever left the great hall for another chamber or den. Someplace where they could ambush her and have the advantage.

But all her plotting was for naught, as Venka stood tall with glazed eyes and drooling lips. Torgerd tried to grab her, but her sweaty hands slid off Venka's arm, and they watched with bated breath as the elf left their hidden refuge and walked into the open to make herself known. The Queen's serpentine head snapped to attention and her blazing eyes zeroed

104

in on the elf. Venka stumbled under the gaze as if she had been struck, but she recovered and continued forward until she stood before Kaigora.

Scaled fingers fluffed Venka's mohawk, a forked tongue slathered her face, and the Queen's body flexed and shuddered. With outrageous ease, she tore off Venka's clothing, and then she fondled the elf's naked body as Venka began to drink the golden liquid that dripped from Kaigora's breasts. The Queen's hands pressed together on Venka's shoulders and elvish bones began to snap.

The disturbing sound woke something in Lorelei and she shook Torgerd.

"This is our moment," she whispered.

Torgerd stared at her as one recovering from a daze. Then she looked back towards the dais as the Queen began to lift Venka into the air. She turned back to Lorelei and gave a short nod.

Kaigora's lips engulfed Venka and she tilted her head backward and began to suck the elf down her stretching gullet. As this was happening, a few of the goahgs began to grunt and snap their jaws in complete shock, as two human women appeared from nowhere and sprinted toward the Queen.

Lorelei reached Kaigora first and her sword sliced across her pale stomach, but a reverberating shock flashed up Lorelei's arms as if she had struck a boulder. Only a small red line showed on Kaigora's skin, and as Lorelei watched, it quickly healed and was no more. The Queen, with her meal only half swallowed, looked down at the small human, and her glare felt like a blast of fiery air as it smote Lorelei.

"Demon," she screamed. And she slashed again and again at Kaigora's bare flesh, causing no lasting damage.

The Queen's jaws clenched and Venka's body was cut in half. Her legs tumbled to the flagstones amid a rush of blood, and the Queen swallowed what remained. Lorelei's shock was quickly forgotten as Kaigora's fist slammed into her chest, tossing her thirty feet across the chamber. Lorelei hit the floor hard, rolled and struggled to breathe, and then vomited a mass of blood. In a daze, she looked up to see goahgs lifting weapons and moving towards her. She fumbled with her sword and it slipped from her moist hands and rang loudly as it hit the stone floor. With a curse she quickly picked it back up as her foes advanced, a mass of taut muscles, scales, and icy reptilian stares.

Nearby, Torgerd now fought with the Queen, and her axe moved in mighty arcs that cut much deeper into Kaigora's flesh, eliciting short shrieks of pain from the serpent's maw. Torgerd dodged the Queen's fist and cut so deep into her thigh that she nearly severed her leg. Kaigora stumbled and her dark blood sprayed the flagstones. Torgerd struck again, hewing into Kaigora's shoulder, sending blood spraying into the air. The serpent's head whipped downward but Torgerd managed to spin clear. She let her momentum carry her, and she threw her arms forward with all the strength she had, and her axe cut deep into the Queen's scaled neck. Kaigora fell to the ground, the floor slick with her blood, and she writhed in pain as death throws coursed through her body.

Farther away in the chamber, Lorelei's sword sheared through a goahg stomach, washing reptilian thighs in blood and bile. The return stroke carried her steel through a reptilian neck, and a third strike cut a goahg face in half. The three bodies twitched in a pile and Lorelei took a step back as more goahgs stepped over their dead kin. The heat and miasma were draining Lorelei quickly. Her arms felt too heavy and her legs were sluggish. She stumbled and reacted too slowly and a goahg sword sliced her arm. Another blade sliced her left leg before she countered to send two more goahgs to the floor with blood leaking from butchered bodies.

A third goahg leapt at her from the top of a treasure mound. Her sword went up and became a stake upon which the goahg impaled itself, but the weight of the creature sent a shock through her shoulders and her injured leg, and she toppled backward with the goahg sprawled across her.

The lizard-like mouth clamped down on her left shoulder and jerked back and forth, determined to rip her apart. Lorelei screamed in pain, and it quickly turned to a cry of desperation as more goahgs approached with jaws snapping and weapons glinting in the chamber light. The savagery in Lorelei's soul boiled up and gave her a renewed burst of energy, and she jammed two fingers from her right hand deep into the goahgs left eye. Fluid from the ruptured organ splashed across Lorelei's face, but she ignored it and pushed harder until the liquid ran red with blood. The goahg released its jaws and pulled its head back to escape. It was a fatal mistake, as Lorelei's freed arm quickly pulled a long dagger and cut the reptile's neck.

Lorelei heaved the dead body to one side and she scrambled to her feet as a throng of goahgs attacked. With sword and dagger, she flailed and slashed like a possessed beast. Blood and scales pooled all around her, while iron and claws cut her clothes and raked her flesh. Before the last goahg fell with its brains rolling down its back, its golden dagger found a home in her side. The reptile twitched at Lorelei's feet and she set her legs wide to keep from falling over. She was drenched in sweat and blood, her enemies and her own. The chamber began to spin before her eyes, but she shook her head and screamed, and her vision refocused. With a quick jerk, she pulled the dagger from her body and tossed it to clatter on the floor.

She glanced towards the dais to see the Serpent Queen floundering on the ground with Torgerd hacking at her bleeding body. Lorelei smiled and turned back towards her next batch of foes, and that is when her scanning eyes saw it. To the left of the dais was a short pile of red gems, and on it sat a golden platter, and upon the platter was an iron crown. It was grey and it did not sparkle, and it was circled by long spikes that stuck out like crude daggers, a symbol of brutality amidst the glittering wealth of the world. It was an object of power, nearly as ancient as Kaigora herself. It was the crown of Kurga, first berserker and eternal consort of the battle god Reh. Kurga, whom Lorelei worshiped above all others. The crown was stolen and then lost ages ago. Kurga searched for it and laid waste to whole kingdoms in her desperate quest to reclaim it. When she followed Lord Reh beyond the mortal realm, her disciples continued to hunt for the lost crown. But none ever learned of its existence, until a faint rumor came to Lorelei on a rainy night as she sacked a tower of wizardry in a remote and forgotten land. That rumor drove her to this pyramid of terror, and the edge of death. But the rumor had proved true. At long last, the crown of Kurga had been found.

Lorelei wiped a bloody hand across her eyes, leaving a crimson smear that mixed with the sweat to run in red rivulets that dripped off her chin. As if in response to her sudden glare, a clump of goahgs formed into a tight group in front of the crown. Anger seethed in Lorelei's heart. How dare they deny her what was rightfully hers. The skin of her neck tingled and she let out a scream of defiance. She charged the goahgs, determined to claim the crown of Kurga, at any cost.

Meanwhile, Torgerd hacked at Kaigora's thick body, cutting deeply through her massive arm muscles. She raised her axe again and stumbled as a crossbow bolt struck her in the stomach. She barely had time to register what had happened, when two more struck her body, one in the lower leg and the other in her upper chest. Torgerd reached down with a steady hand and pulled the bolt from her stomach. Blood ran from the wound and down over her thighs, a bright river that reflected the sparkling light around it. Two goahgs suddenly came at her from behind and their daggers slashed her back. She spun about and her axe hewed off one head. The second goahg jumped forward and its jaws clamped onto Torgerd's neck. She dropped her axe and grabbed the goahg's throat with both hands. She felt the sharp reptilian teeth pierce her flesh, and she could feel the dagger in its hand as it repeatedly stabbed her defenseless body.

Lorelei hacked at her foes with growing desperation and madness as she slowly moved closer to the iron crown. Scaled limbs were severed from naked reptilian bodies, fanged muzzles were hewn in half, breasts were cut apart, and innards tumbled to the floor and mixed with brain matter and seeping gore. In their death throes the goahgs would cling to Lorelei to allow their kin openings to strike. Lorelei was cut and bitten several times during the melee, but after several hard minutes, she found herself alone, surrounded by the butchered remains of the reptiles. In that moment of respite, she glanced at her companion and became aware of her terrible plight.

"Torgerd, stand fast!" screamed Lorelei in a panic. Then she was beset again by fresh enemies which forced her focus away from her struggling friend.

The muscles on Torgerd's arms bulged and clamped down as hard as they could, causing the goahg's throat to collapse. Its jaws loosened and came free. Torgerd tossed the reptile to the floor, retrieved her axe, and hacked the squirming beast in half. She touched the numerous bleeding teeth holes around her neck and cursed, but she ignored the fresh dagger punctures that circled her body, refusing to die at the hand of a foul lizard man. She was a proud daughter of the North, blessed by the great gods of ice and snow. The strength of her kin burned bright in her veins and she raised her axe high and laughed with a clear and wholesome voice, untainted by the horrors that surrounded her.

"Hahaha, demons of Hel, the North Wind has come to crack your scales and break your foul souls! I wash this hellscape with your brains, and I laugh at your feebleness. Woe to any reptile bastard that would challenge me! Come, you scaly fiends! You face Torgerd, daughter of Bulgur the Brave, and hammer of the seven clans of Azgard. Come to your death!"

Lorelei finished hacking through a lizard neck and she raised her bloody sword towards Torgerd and cheered. But the joyful cry died on her lips and her heart sank. For in that moment of victory and mirth, the Serpent Queen rose from the floor, fully healed and full of wrath.

Kaigora towered over Torgerd and her terrible muscles flexed with unbridled rage and her serpentine neck swayed back and forth while her yellow eyes beat down on the red-headed barbarian. The black viper's head struck with staggering speed, a spear tip of such cruelty and power that no champion had ever withstood it. Kaigora's long teeth sank deep into Torgerd's torso. Her snake lips rippled about, cutting wider wounds, and seeking even deeper purchase. Torgerd still held her axe, but her arm was pinned by the great jaws. Her other arm feebly pushed against the ebony scales that held her tight. The Queen lifted the barbarian and casually glared across the chamber at Lorelei. A hissing chuckle somehow escaped her clenched jaws.

With a mouth full of blood, Torgerd wailed and moaned, before being thrown to the floor with bone-crushing power. Kaigora's long tongue tasted Torgerd's moaning face and then her mountainous arms began to rain blow after blow on her defeated enemy.

Lorelei began to run to Torgerd's aid, but she suddenly stopped and turned back in a moment of indecision. The crown of Kurga was unguarded. A quick dash and she could have it. She looked towards her friend being pummeled by Kaigora and then she looked again at the beckoning crown of iron. Her uncertainty was cut short by pain as a crossbow bolt pierced her side. Another cut her cheek and nearly took out an eye. A third cut her chest and was luckily turned away by her collarbone before it could sink home in her neck. Six goahgs with crossbows formed a line thirty yards away and they kept firing at her. More lizard men stalked behind them with snapping jaws and broad cleavers. Lorelei turned from the assault and her tired legs felt like lead as she sprinted towards the Serpent Queen and her fallen sister.

Kaigora was ready for her, and as Lorelei raised her sword to strike, a fist like iron crushed her between the breasts. She hit the floor hard and struggled to regain her breath, fearing that her bones had been shattered. Kaigora lunged and Lorelei barely avoided the striking head of death, rolling away at the last instant. She lashed out with her sword and cut a shallow mark across the serpent's head. Kaigora laughed at the impotence of this blonde warrior, and she began to chant in some abhorrent forgotten language. The goahgs snapped their jaws in unison and moaned in deep guttural voices, creating a cacophony of madness that echoed through the chamber.

Lorelei grabbed Torgerd by the vest and began to drag her away from the Queen. A ghastly smear of blood was left in the wake of the body. Kaigora casually moved to follow them, her serpentine head sinking low so that her forked tongue could taste the blood trail. Lorelei leapt forward with her sword pointing at the Queen.

"You will not touch her again!" screamed Lorelei.

A flash of black and a quick snap, and Kaigora's jaws broke Lorelei's sword and engulfed her sword hand. The berserker screamed as she was pulled forward and then lifted off the floor. But a quick jerk of the Queen's powerful head sent Lorelei tumbling across the floor with a bloody stump where her hand used to be. Lorelei writhed in pain and grabbed at her right forearm above the severed mess as it spouted blood in torrents. With only moments to live, Lorelei staggered towards a nearby brazier that billowed with flames, and with a terrible scream, she pressed her wound against the red-hot steel that circled the fire. She gritted her teeth and nearly passed out as her flesh was burnt and cauterized. Tears ran down her cheeks, her body shook from the trauma of so much pain, and the smell of her cooking flesh made her vomit, but she kept her arm on the metal until she was certain that the bleeding had mostly stopped. She fell to the floor and moaned in anguish. With a shaking hand, she tied her shirt sleeve over her smoking stump, as if the cloth would provide some comfort.

Through the haze of tears and exhaustion, Lorelei could see the Queen flexing with triumph as she strutted towards her. Black-scaled hands caressed her aroused breasts and they rubbed over massively

111

muscled thighs, and then they massaged the serpent neck as it swayed in the golden light.

"Human fool," hissed the Queen in an alluring voice. "You cannot harm me. You are nothing. I am eternal life and eternal power. What are you to me? I discovered the elder serpents as they slept amidst the blood of the ancient world. I built this temple paradise for them with my own hands. I devoured the oldest races of the West. The wealth of the world is mine! I bathe in the finest oils from hidden fairy lands, I mate with whomever I desire, I am feared and loved, and all beings of this world are mine to feast upon whenever I wish. I am the last elven goddess to walk this mortal realm. I am unbreakable and everlasting. In my great presence, you are inadequate in every way, simple savage. So, what are you to me? I will torture you slowly before I eat you, lowly bastard human. I will flay your skin and lay waste to your soul, and you will bow to me willingly before I give you eternal peace in my stomach."

One word from Kaigora's taunts caught Lorelei's ear and she looked about frantically till she saw her salvation. Not far away was a broad empty pool, and near it were many jars with tight caps. Lorelei ran for the jars and the Serpent Queen merely watched curiously.

"There is nowhere to flee, mouse," laughed Kaigora.

Lorelei grabbed a midsized jar, pulled off the cap, and smiled. She spun about in a circle to gain momentum, and then she released the jar and sent it flying toward the Queen. The trajectory carried it over the brazier, and a single finger of flame was all it took to light the oil in the jar. Kaigora's eyes went wide and her laughter stopped as the jar exploded into a mass of fiery liquid that splashed across her torso. She batted at the flames but they clung to her and burned her skin and engulfed her black hands.

Lorelei tossed two more jars across the floor to smash and catch fire in front of the startled Queen, creating a wall of fire between the serpent and the humans. A final burst of adrenaline gripped Lorelei and she lifted Torgerd over her shoulder and carried her from the chamber of death while the Queen raged and screamed beyond the flames.

The maze-like corridors of the pyramid with their many rooms and alcoves had provided comforting hiding spots, but now they held terror and uncertainty, and with every random path she chose, Lorelei feared she would meet goahgs or other monsters. Too weak and vulnerable to defend herself, they would kill her easily. For many unbearably tense minutes, she struggled onwards, until passing through several small rooms and short curving hallways, she found a small dusty anti-chamber in the back of a dark room filled with moldy statuary. The chamber had a thick door and the room itself appeared to be seldom visited. She laid Torgerd in the anti-chamber and pulled the door shut, and then she collapsed. Lorelei cradled her butchered arm in the folds of her blood-soaked shirt, and she laid her remaining hand on her friend's forehead, weeping as quietly as she could until she finally passed out from pain and blood loss.

10. Glory

Clawed feet scurried across stone tiles and the scratching caused Lorelei to wake with a start from her tortured slumber. Her body was stiff and she struggled to move. Next to her lay Torgerd, pale and cold. She was dead. Miraculously, she still clutched her axe tightly in one hand, a sign of her fierce defiance in the face of death. Lorelei brushed some red hairs away from Torgerd's battered peaceful face. Then she cautiously opened the door to the small chamber where she hid. The room beyond was quiet and devoid of enemies. She staggered into it and nearly fell over, her head swimming, and her legs shaking. She steadied herself against a dusty wall and then began to search its many niches and adjoining rooms. After a few minutes, her search was rewarded, and she found a large clean jar next to a small fountain of cold flowing water. She stuck her head in the fountain and then drank deeply, the water acting like a healing salve to her dry throat. It gave her energy and cleared the haze from her pounding head. She filled the jar, carried it back to the anti-chamber, and sat down next to Torgerd's body, closing the door once again.

She drank some more, then studied her ruined arm, remembering the terrible moment when she had lost her hand. She cradled it close to her body and gripped Torgerd's cold arm with her remaining fingers. No doubt, Kaigora's burns had healed by now and she was once again holding court in her hedonistic chamber of gold and terror. Thinking about the Serpent Queen sent shivers down Lorelei's spine and the hairs on her neck prickled with fear. It was a deep-rooted fear she had never known before. For the first time in her life, she was unsure she could defeat an enemy. She imagined herself being abused and tortured by the Queen's gaudily muscled form. She could feel the hot moist folds of Kaigora's throat as it closed around her body and pulled her down to a slow, dark death.

Lorelei lashed out and pounded the wall, ashamed of her failure and fears.

The waves of despair rolled over her, threatening to drown her in death, and in that moment of hopelessness, a voice came to her. She froze, afraid that she had been discovered by the Queen's minions. Her keen ears listened intently for the slightest sound, and a gravely, comforting voice whispered to her.

"Hail, berserker," said Zuda, her old mentor.

"Z-Zuda?" questioned Lorelei. "Is it really you? Has your spirit come to haunt me? Have you come to look upon my failure?"

"Why do you cower?" asked Zuda. "Why do you hide like a mouse? You are stronger than this."

"I am not stronger than Kaigora. The serpent has eldritch power that cannot be broken. She is invincible."

"Hahaha," laughed Zuda slowly. "You have much to learn, young slayer. The berserker will always be stronger than any foe. The berserker is life. It is the struggle to survive, at any cost. It is chaos and passion. The heart of the berserker is stronger than any creature, including this one. Release the berserker, Lorelei goat-herder."

"I am maimed," said Lorelei, lifting her stump. "I am no longer whole."

"One arm or two, it matters not," said Zuda. "You sacked the dome of Likantos and butchered the mad wolf within. You slew the minotaur of Grull, killed the Red Knights of Drunlan, and hacked apart the brigand army in the hills of Jerika. You did not do these things because you had two hands. Cower in the shadows no longer! Be who you are meant to be! Release the berserker!"

"Yes," said Lorelei with a mad gleam in her eye. With her one hand, she tore her shirt open and pulled it off, exposing her naked torso to the darkness.

"Let Kurga protect you," whispered Zuda. "Let her power be your shield. Where is the fire and passion? Where is the warrior I trained? Where is Kurga's daughter? Show her the chaos in your heart."

Lorelei pulled off her boots, and with growing urgency, she stripped off her pants and tossed them aside with an angry grunt.

"Be free of the serpent's madness!" growled Zuda. "Release the berserker!"

Zuda's voice trailed off into the ether with his last plea and Lorelei knelt solemnly before the body of Torgerd. Sweat began to bead up on her naked skin, and she rubbed her hand across her strong arms, stomach, and thighs, reconnecting with her flesh. Finally, she touched the skull tattoos on her chest.

"Mighty Kurga," whispered Lorelei into the blackness. "I will face the serpent again, as your true disciple, revealed in glory on the field of battle. I will bring your power down upon the black scales of Kaigora and test their mettle one last time. I will not retreat again, I swear it."

Lorelei crouched over Torgerd's body. "I will return for you, sister," she said. And then she touched Torgerd's side, which was still slick with blood, and with a crimson palm, she gripped her own left breast. She grabbed the battle axe and stood tall, with vengeance seething in her heart.

"We finish this fight together, daughter of the North," she said, before kissing the axe blade.

With confidence, Lorelei strutted out of the room and moved through the putrid corridors, eager to slay and lay waste to all the demons of this citadel of horror. She stalked the catacombs unmolested until she found a small room near a wide junction where several corridors met. She could hear much scurrying and shuffling about down the various dark pathways, and the noise lifted her grim spirits. She smirked, stepped back into the shadows of the room, and waited, like a lion in tall grass.

Kaigora lay restlessly on her mountain of cushions. She had not felt such anger and hate for a long age of the world, and she lusted to taste the escaped savage with her cruel tongue. This human would suffer long for her audacity. The Queen's spiteful eyes shifted towards a group of swagoab guards who marched into her chamber, their golden cloaks concealing their deformed bodies except for their bowing reptilian heads. Among them were half a dozen naked dwarves, dirty and shivering with fear.

The Queen walked forward slowly, her every step a prelude to violence, and her serpentine neck shook with the anger that she could barely contain. The lead swagoab bowed low and offered the dwarves to his Queen. With a reverberating hiss, she reached out a hand and stroked his lizard-like face. And with a sudden flex of her powerful arm, she crushed the swagoab's head. Its body jerked briefly before hanging limp, its brains and pulverized bones dripping from between the Queen's clenched hand. The other swagoab guards bowed even lower in an attempt to appease her wrath.

The dwarves moaned with fright and several urinated uncontrollably onto the floor. Kaigora slowly reached out her long neck, scales flashing in the trembling light of the treasure chamber. Her broad smooth lips snatched the first dwarf and quickly swallowed him. His muffled screams could be heard as he slid down her monstrous gullet. A flash of black, and the next dwarf was impaled on her fangs, and then quickly swallowed. Kaigora flexed her terrible muscles and screamed in anger, and her fist smashed the stone floor, breaking the rock as if it was rotted wood. Her viper head struck again and she bit deep into another swagoab soldier. As it dangled from her mouth, she tore off its limbs and then flung the corpse onto a pile of golden coins. Her forked tongue licked the blood from her scaled lips and flicked gently as her head hovered over the assemblage, casting a shadow of death that touched all creatures equally. With unquenched wrath, she continued to eat dwarves and kill her followers in a grotesque display of wanton butchery.

When all the dwarves had been eaten, three swagoab remained, and they slowly backed away from the Queen. She hissed death and paced about her dais, flexing with rage. Suddenly, Kaigora stopped pacing and she turned to glare at one swagoab soldier who was not with the other three. This guard stood opposite to its brethren, and though its head was bowed, its bearing was not that of a supplicant. The Queen hissed and her eyes beat upon the guard, but that terrible hiss ended sharply as the swagoab pulled back its golden cloak to reveal the hard-muscled body of a naked human woman, with blonde pubic hair, skull tattoos on her upper chest, and a crimson hand print on her breast.

The cloak fell away completely, and a steady hand reached up and peeled back the folds of the lizard's neck skin to reveal a face with hard piercing emerald eyes. Finally, the reptilian head, which had been worn like a grisly helmet, was tossed aside. The woman shook out her slick hair, stained and soaked with the blood of the goahg she had impersonated. Lizard blood dripped onto her thick shoulders and small breasts, and it ran in streaks down her smiling face as she glared at the Queen defiantly. The golden rings in her nose sparkled and the reflection of them in her green eyes was like lightning.

Kaigora tilted her head in stunned silence as she studied this strange human. In her one hand, she held a familiar battle axe, and Kaigora's eyes bulged with anger when she finally noticed the burnt stump where the woman's other hand should have been.

Lorelei had slowly moved across the chamber while Kaigora ate and slew in her violent tantrum until she stood near a specific pile of gems and the precious treasure that lay upon it. Now revealed to her enemy, Lorelei dropped her axe on the floor, breaking the dread silence with a sharp clang. She turned to her left and grabbed the iron crown of Kurga. She placed it on her head with reverence, and the last effects of the Queen's miasma suddenly fell away. The crown was like a lightning rod to Lorelei's soul. Her limbs filled with power and her mind with clear purpose. She hefted her axe and barked savagely as the remaining swagoab charged her, their golden cloaks flowing behind as they ran.

With only a few strokes she laid waste to the fiends and wetted the floor with their guts. Her naked feet stepped over their twitching bodies, moving towards the Queen with a bold and confident stride, a hunter stalking its prey.

"I am Lorelei Tyrsdotir," she declared. "Berserker of Kurga."

"Human wretch," spit Kaigora between hisses.

"I have come to slay thee, Queen of Serpents," cooed Lorelei with a mad grin. "For the glory of Kurga, I spill your blood."

In mere seconds the Queen was upon Lorelei, head striking, fists pounding, with anger rumbling from her body like a hellish drum. The berserker met her foe with unparalleled ferocity. She dodged and weaved the killing strikes with cat-like speed, and all the while, her axe slashed back and forth. Bloody seams began to spread across Kaigora's mass, and the more that appeared, the slower they healed.

With an aggressive lunge, Lorelei cut deep into the corner of Kaigora's open mouth, shearing through teeth, gums, and then scale-covered flesh. Kaigora pulled back quickly as dark blood filled her mouth. Lorelei pressed her attack and cut down through Kaigora's nearest scaled foot, splitting the appendage down the middle, like a log made of flesh. The Queen shrieked and her hand crashed into Lorelei's face, sending her sprawling.

Lorelei rolled into a crouch, blood dripping from her snarling lips. The Queen attacked again and threw her awesome weight behind a punch meant to crush Lorelei's bones into gory mush. In response, the speed of the berserker's axe was blinding and it bit deep, completely severing Kaigora's right hand. The Queen's viperous head flashed but only glanced off Lorelei's spinning hip. The axe cut again, through the black scales of Kaigora's neck. The Queen stumbled backward as her blood sprayed from the pink wound, covering Lorelei in the crimson life force of the ancient demigod. Kaigora's neck coiled in retreat and she sought distance to recover from the berserker's assault.

Lorelei, drenched in blood and sweat, foamed at the mouth and she slapped her firm chest and barked like a wolf gone completely mad. She looked down at the Queen's severed hand and saw an obscene sight; the tendons and muscles of the hand stretched and moved, trying to find Kaigora's arm so they could reattach themselves. A wild instinct screamed inside Lorelei's brain, and with her axe, she cut open the burnt flesh of her own severed arm. She fell to her knees and with halting breaths she offered her own mutilated stump to the searching black-scaled hand. Greedily, Kaigora's flesh took the offering, and slithering muscles sunk deep into Lorelei's arm. Cramps wracked her powerful muscles and she fought hard to breathe, but after a few moments of intense pain, Lorelei raised her new right hand and watched with joy as its scaled surface reflected the glittering gems of the chamber. Laughter flowed from her throat and she spun the axe back and forth between her two hands, testing the strength of the serpent's grip.

Her mirth turned to a simmering battle-lust and she looked upon the cowering Serpent Queen, whose neck still squirted blood. Her imposing form had lost its vibrancy and aura, and her muscles quivered with pain as the seeping neck wound spit crimson streams all down her body. The loss of her hand was one wound too far, her great healing abilities stretched past their formidable limits.

Lorelei barked again and her naked thighs exploded with power as she launched herself at Kaigora, axe spinning in the glittering light. A gash opened across Kaigora's arm, and before she could counter, another great fissure split open across her iron stomach. Black blood and dark intestines rushed to the floor. Lorelei's corded muscles strained with power and the axe hacked through the bone and sinew between Kaigora's breasts, embedding itself deeply. The black head speared forward and Lorelei caught it with her hands. She roared as she held the jaws closed, fighting against the last strength of the dying Serpent Queen. Lorelei leaned in close, and with a sudden head-butt, she pierced Kaigora's golden eye with a spike from her iron crown. The viper's head shook violently, but Lorelei held fast, pivoted, and pulled Kaigora down to the floor. Then, using Kaigora's own black hand as a spear, she stabbed her arm into the ruptured eye as far as it would go.

The berserker ripped her arm free of its fleshy scabbard and she pounded her chest with the gore-soaked appendage, roaring like a demonic lion. Kaigora feebly tried to move about, but her strength had left her. Lorelei retrieved her axe from Kaigora's chest, and she stood before the floundering Queen in the light of the serpent's remaining eye. She ran her black-scaled blood-soaked hand across her body, scratched at her pubic hair, and then tapped the large skull tattoo on her chest.

"I am Kurga's daughter, great Queen of nothingness," she spat. She raised her arms above her head and smiled as blood dripped off the axe to hit her chin and roll down her breasts, caressing her nipples. "I am the one true berserker, immune to your hate and wickedness. You are broken, serpent. I sampled your power and have found it less than my own."

Lorelei's wet muscles glistened as the axe fell over and over until the butchery was complete. The victorious berserker lifted the severed serpent head high and then tossed it far from the black neck, which writhed about and pumped blood in gouts across the floor. Lorelei's naked feet waded through the spreading puddle and left crimson prints across the flagstones as she slowly walked from the treasure chamber.

She returned a few minutes later, carrying Torgerd's body. She carefully placed her friend on a mound of golden coins and fiery gems. Then she put the great axe on her chest, and she kissed the barbarian one last time.

"You go to the halls of the great warriors," said Lorelei as fresh tears ran down her cheeks. "Hold your head high, sister. Your deed will be legendary, even among the gods."

Lorelei poured oil upon Torgerd, and upon the gems and the gold, and she coated Kaigora's quivering corpse. She smashed all the oil jars she could find and she piled up all the tapestries and banners from adjoining rooms. In a nearby chamber, there were great piles of wood used to keep the braziers lit, and Lorelei toiled for hours until all the dry kindling had been tossed into the treasure room. Finally, she gathered up two sacks of gold for herself, and then she lit a torch in a brazier and tossed it towards the oil-soaked dais. Half the chamber lit instantly in a flash of glorious light that burnt away the darkness of that dread hall.

"Kurga," yelled Lorelei, "let the fire burn long and hot! Honor this warrior for me. Please."

As the inferno raged and grew, Lorelei carried her bags of treasure out of the pyramid. She was greeted by Woden, whose body was splashed with blood, for he had fulfilled his role, smashing many goahgs in the field of moss.

The fresh air felt good as it caressed Lorelei's naked body, and she laughed. She slung the treasure and her traveling pack across the rhino's broad back. Then she mounted him and together they rode away as black smoke billowed from the holes on the pyramid's surface.

The fire burned for days until the ancient stones crumbled into a great slag heap. A mighty tomb for a great warrior.

END

Art by Max Fuchs
Instagram @themaxfuchs

For more of Lorelei's
adventures, please refer
to the author's website:

www.bludgeonedtodeath.com

And be sure to check out the official
Berserker soundtrack by Orcus.
Released by HDK, Find it at:

heimatderkatastrophe.bandcamp.com/music
Instagram @heimat_der_katastrophe
@orcus.ds

www.ingramcontent.com/pod-product-compliance
Lightning Source LLC
Chambersburg PA
CBHW030631130626
46552CB00002B/793